I0762203

THE WAYS WE GET BY

THE WAYS WE GET BY

JOE DORNICH

www.blacklawrence.com

Executive Editor: Diane Goettel
Book and Cover Design: Zoe Norvell
Cover Art: "Smeared Lipstick III, 11x15" by Deb Weiers

ISBN: 978-1-62557-132-8

Published 2020 by Black Lawrence Press.

FOR MY MOM

SORRY ABOUT ALL OF THE SWEAR WORDS.

CONTENTS

The Continuing Controversy of the Snuggle Shack

Lonnie calls and tells me my first session isn't until noon, which is great because it means the protestors will be on their lunch break and not there to remind me that I'm a Hell-bound gigolo. And a murderer. Of course, when I get to work there is a woman who has apparently brown-bagged it. She is perched on the curb with her protest sign across her lap, slowly destroying what appears to be an egg salad sandwich. She must spot my Snuggle Shack employee T-shirt, which advertises me as a "Certified Cuddler," because she bolts to attention, holding her sign high and proud. In bold, red letters, it reads: SNUGGLE SLUTS GO HOME! I want to ask this woman if she really thinks this is where I want to be. If she truly believes this is the life I always imagined for myself. But I don't. I just smile weakly and compliment her use of alliteration.

Across the street, I see a giant hulk of a man, like an armoire with limbs. He's balding on the sides, and all the way bald up top, and the midday sun glints off of his huge, smooth dome. At first, I think he's just another protestor, but he isn't holding a sign or telling me what a terrible person I am. He just stares. He stares right at me. Then the woman beside me starts screaming something about how I'm unraveling the fabric of this great and noble country, but it's hard to make out because her mouth is full of egg salad. I ignore them both and go inside.

Upstairs, I find Lonnie in his office meditating beneath his eight watercolors of the Dalai Lama, and the photo of himself and Stanley Geegland. Stanley is Lonnie's friend from rehab who bears an uncanny resemblance to Bono. He even wears the little rose-colored glasses. Mindy and Allison, our two female snugglers, are in awe of the photo, and while Lonnie never outright says it's Bono, he doesn't correct them either. If Lonnie is aware of my presence, he doesn't acknowledge it. I knock on the door jamb, interrupting what I'm sure is his inevitable Transcendence Into Enlightenment. Lonnie opens his eyes. He asks if my time away was mentally and spiritually recuperative. He asks if I am prepared to continue doing the healing work of Touch Therapy.

I say sure to both.

"I certainly hope so," Lonnie says. "The file is on the desk." Then he closes his eyes and continues his pursuit of Zen.

My first client of the day is one Sara Mews. According to her Snuggle Scenario, we'll spend an hour in the Etruscan Room, on the bed, but above the covers. She has opted out of the Ambient Aural Therapy, which is great because that includes the Maui Waterfalls Fountain. That thing always makes me have to pee. Her file tells me that Sara suffers from social anxiety and mild depression. Her intake photo shows a thin, middle-aged woman who looks like she's never smiled in her life. I've seen mug shots with more glee. Even so, she's my first client since the incident, and I can't afford another suspension. Under her Preferred Therapy Postures, Sara has said that she'd like to start as the Little Spoon but is open to some possible Face-to-Face. So that's how we begin.

Though Lonnie officially runs The Snuggle Shack, his dad is bankrolling it. Mr. Johnson made his fortune inventing that white foam tray beef is sold on. I guess before then meat was just wrapped in butcher paper, and the blood and other juices would leak out. Johnson's Meat Trays absorb those carnivorous reminders, and now they're in every deli and supermarket in the country. Mindy, Allison, and I call him the Meat Diaper Man, though never in front of Lonnie.

The story is that a few years ago, Lonnie was living with a vet tech and, at some point, became addicted to Canine Oxycodone. He did a few failed stints in rehab, but the last one had more of a holistic, mind-body type of approach. Lots of touch therapy and elephant gods. Whatever it was, it worked, and Lonnie's been gulping the Energy Exchange Kool-Aid ever since. He promised Dad he'd stay clean if, in return, he'd help turn his new interests into a business. Lonnie used the money to convert the offices of a defunct law firm into three Snuggle Suites, each with a couch, pillow-top bed, adjustable lighting, and those ambient nature CDs. Though we've only been open a few months, and some people are coming around to the idea of Contact Medicine, most of the town thinks we're running some kind of new-age brothel.

My session with Sara does not go well. During Big/Little Spoon, my arm keeps falling asleep, and strands of her hair drift into my mouth. I sneeze an unacceptable number of times. Though she remains stoically silent, I can tell Sara would be more relaxed if she were being buried alive. I suggest we try some Face-to-Face. This is a mistake. Snuggle Protocol requires that Face-to-Face include prolonged periods of therapeutic stroking along the shoulders and back area. Normally this is fine, but Sara has a number of pronounced moles on her back, like God, or Jesus, or whoever, super-glued a handful of Raisinets back there before forcing her into this world. Every time I begin one of my stroking maneuvers, I run up against one of Sara's moles and stop short. I'm afraid of accidently lopping one off. Instead, I resort to a series of tentative, gentle pats that probably have little therapeutic value. It's like frisking a baby. Sara's disappointment is profound. Her mouth curls down, deepening already prominent frown lines. Her eyes stare at me with the lidless disinterest of a reptile. It doesn't help that our faces are about six inches apart. My Snuggle Summary Evaluation does not look promising.

It doesn't take long. I'm sanitizing the slippers with disinfectant spray when Allison tells me Lonnie wants to see me in his office.

He's still in the lotus position when I arrive.

"Take a seat please," he says.

There are no chairs in Lonnie's office, just a bunch of meditation pillows and a few yoga mats. I move to sit on a purple and gold cushion, but Lonnie says no. He means I should sit on the floor. So I sit on the floor.

"I, we, all of us here are in the business of healing," he says. "And while of course the healing is our main objective, we depend on the business component to provide this service. The lights don't run on love, do they? I can't pay the rent on this place with smiles, can I?"

I admit that he cannot.

"So, until we all live in some kind of utopia where love and smiles are the primary means of commerce, we need the business. And that means clients. But you, you are driving those clients away from here, and in one case, right out of existence. At least, on this plane anyway."

Lonnie's talking about the woman I killed. Mrs. Dorothy Simone. Technically, she died of "natural causes," but that's a detail a number of people seem to be ignoring. Like the protestors. Like Lonnie.

"Each of us," he continues, "is striving for spiritual completeness. To find that harmonious balance between ourselves and our surroundings. We do this even though we know the journey will never end. Even though we know we will never be completely whole. Perhaps I've overestimated your position on this journey. Maybe, given your current level of wholeness, being a healing influence on others is asking too much. Does this make sense?"

I nod. I nod and try to ignore that fact that I'm having my "wholeness" judged by a guy who was once addicted to puppy smack.

"However," Lonnie says, "despite the unfortunate scene with Mrs. Simone, she did like you. As do the rest of our advanced clientele."

He means old people.

"So, until further notice, they will make up your client list. I will handle everyone else, as well as any walk-ins. Mindy and Allison, per usual, will take care of our male clientele."

"And when I'm not embracing the elderly," I say, "then what? What about the rest of my shift?"

"Equally divided between Maintenance and Housekeeping."

"C'mon, Lonnie, you know I can't afford to change sheets all day. I need the tips."

"Then allow me to give you the most valuable tip of all," he says. "Unburden yourself from this negativity that is blocking your spiritual growth. Develop a calming, peaceful center, and allow it to expand and radiate out to others. Because, if you can't, you'll never know true serenity. Plus, I'll fire you."

Then Lonnie dismisses me, but not before giving me a copy of my Written Warning, which highlights the changes to my shifts. Lonnie's signed the bottom, and I notice he's dotted the *i* with a tiny yin and yang symbol.

A little piece inside of me dies.

I go back to work.

Mrs. Dorothy Simone was my regular nine-thirty Thursdays. She was a sweet old lady, though a bit eccentric. Always showed up for our session with her face completely made up, wearing full jewelry and some sequined ball gown like she was off to celebrate the repeal of Prohibition. I'd remind Mrs. Simone that we couldn't snuggle with her dressed like that, and she'd bring a manicured hand to an overly rouged cheek and feign embarrassment. *You know*, she'd say, *if you want me to slip into something more comfortable, all you have to do is ask.* Then she'd call me "troublesome" and I'd give her a pair of the pajamas we keep on hand for the lawyers and businesspeople who come in on their lunch breaks and don't want to wrinkle their suits.

We went through this routine every Thursday.

The day it happened, Mrs. Simone and I were snuggling on the couch in the Stillwater Room as usual, and after some time, she put her head in my lap and I ran a brush through her sparse, pewter-colored hair. She fell asleep, leaving a drool stain on my pants that looked like an upside-down South America. I didn't mind. When our session ended, I tried to gently shake Mrs. Simone awake. Then I used a little more force. Still, I got no response. Of course Lonnie freaked, though, to me, slipping away in a painless, peaceful slumber seems like the utmost degree of relaxation, and something of a testament to my abilities as a Snuggler. Few saw it that way. Mindy wrote "The Cuddling Kevorkian" on my locker in red lipstick. Lonnie had to call for a shutdown and bribe the EMTs to take Mrs. Simone's body out the back. Even so, the protestors got wind of it, and now they have a whole other reason to hate us. We all got sent home early, which meant lost revenue, and more than a few unpleasant looks in my direction. Did anyone ask if I was okay? If I suffered any residual trauma from having a woman die in my lap? They did not. Was I praised for not mentioning the fact I wouldn't be receiving my usual twenty percent tip? I was not. What I did get was three days Reflective Suspension. I thought about quitting. Then I thought about the shameful six months of trying to shop around my degree in Television History and the realization that I am unqualified for just about every job out there.

I'm in Laundry, trying to wrestle the duvets back into the duvet covers, when Lonnie sticks his head in and says phone. It's Gloria, the live-in I hired for Gramps. She says we have a problem. She says I need to come home right away. In the background, I hear Gramps screaming that he's going to be late. Something made of glass breaks. I tell Gloria I'll be right there.

"I have an emergency at home," I say to Lonnie, "but I'll be back as soon as I can." He reminds me to breathe and focus on my bliss.

Outside, the protestors have returned from lunch en masse. When they spot me, their faces screw up in identical grimaces of judgment. They shout and shake their signs—DOWN WITH COMPANION$HIP, A-LONE IS BETTER THAN A-JOHN—in my face, as if hoping to fling some of their righteous wisdom on me.

Across the street is the balding armoire man from earlier. His body goes rigid when he sees me, and his faces mottles like ground beef. He moves to cross the street, ignoring or oblivious to the cars that have to stop short to keep from slamming into him. Just as he's about to reach me, a man steps between us. He says that I, and the work I do, are affronts to the Lord. His tongue darts in and out of his mouth when he speaks, and flecks of spittle land on my shirt. He holds a sign with a Bible verse written on it, and though I don't know it specifically, I imagine it refers to my wayward soul and the eternal Hell-fires that will eventually consume it. The man says that I need to atone for my sinful ways, and accept Christ into my life, just as he has. Then he bops me on the head with the cardboard end of his sign.

I rush home.

When I arrive, I find Gloria chasing Gramps around the loveseat. Gramps is wearing his navy-blue pinstripe suit. Gloria looks more flustered than usual.

"I'm going to be late," Gramps says when he sees me. "This... woman here is making me very late."

On the floor, shattered into a dozen pieces, is one of Mom's Adorable Occasions figurines. It is, was, a calf and a tiger cub on a teeter-totter. I never liked that one. It never made sense to me, biologically speaking. Sure, maybe their friendship works for a while because they're young and don't know any better. But once that tiger cub grows up and realizes where he fits in this world, and what's expected of him, he's going to pounce off that teeter-totter and turn that calf into veal and wallets.

"What are you going to be late for?" I ask Gramps.

"Work of course. I have to be at the office by nine."

"No," I say. "You don't. You don't have to work anymore. You're retired."

Gramps looks around the room, and then at Gloria and me as if we've invaded his dreams. "I am?" he says.

"Yeah," I say. I take Gramps by the arm and lead him to his bedroom. His hands are trembling, and I help him remove his suit jacket and loosen his tie. It's amazing. Most of the time the poor guy has no idea where he is, or what's going on, but he can still tie the cleanest Half-Windsor I've ever seen. I'm grateful for these lightning flashes of lucidity, even as they remind me of Gramps's daily darkness.

"This is not working," Gloria says as she sweeps up porcelain animal pieces.

"I know," I say, "and I'm sorry. I know he's been challenging lately, but there's a new medication, and maybe..."

"No, not just the Señor," Gloria says. "You and I. I have not been paid in three weeks. I cannot afford."

"Please. Just give me a few more days. Here," I say as I pull out my wallet, immediately and painfully aware of the futility of this gesture. I open it, hoping I guess that the pair of dollar bills inside have mated and reproduced. No such luck.

"Take this," I tell her. "I'll have some more for you soon."

But Gloria just stares at my meager offering and smiles. She spends more on bus fare coming out here.

"I'm sorry," she says. "I cannot." Then she hands me the broom, grabs her purse, and walks out.

I stand at the window, hoping Gloria will change her mind or at least glance back at us one more time. She does neither. Gloria becomes, along with Sara Mews, the second woman today to walk out on me filled with disappointment.

I'm on a roll.

I microwave some hot dogs for dinner, and Gramps and I settle in to watch his favorite show, *Pre-K MMA*. We're just in time for the main event. The announcer says today's bout features the toughest tots this side of the Mississippi: "Tiger" Timmy Witherspoon versus Preston "The Blade" Dempsey. The Tiger looks big for his age. Gramps suspects him of doping. The fight is less mixed martial arts and more of an arms flailing, windmill type of exchange. The Blade has some good moves, but his head is too big for his body, and it keeps throwing him off balance. A couple of times the Tiger wanders off in the wrong direction and the ref has to reset.

"Your mother came to visit me last night," Gramps says in between bites of hot dog.

This is an impressive bit of news as Mom's been dead almost a year now.

"Really," I say. "How's she look?"

"She's worried about you. She thinks you spend too much time alone. She wants you to meet a nice girl."

"Well," I say, "if you two somehow talk again, tell her I'm fine. Tell her I'm not lonely. I meet nice girls every day."

We watch the rest of the fight. In the third round, The Blade trips on his own feet and bites his tongue. He cries on the mat until the ref counts him down, and the Tiger wins by Technical Knockout, and that's that.

I'm back at work on Tuesday, which is when the van arrives from Renaissance Gardens. The RG is a top-tier assisted living facility. I'd love to move Gramps there, but that place takes some serious bucks. I can't even afford the warped linoleum and wet bacon smells of Wavering Meadows. The protestors are pretty well behaved on Tuesdays, as most people are usually reluctant to yell at the elderly. Sure, some people still shake their signs and chant how "Hugs Beget Whoredom," but most find it tough to sling their condemnation at someone's Bubby while she hobbles past in her pink housecoat.

I've brought Gramps to The Shack with me. It seemed like the best way to keep him out of trouble. Allison says she'll help keep an eye on him and maybe work in a free Snuggle Session if there's time. Allison is great. She's my girl, or she would be if she only realized how much we had in common. Her dad left, too, walking out on her and her mother and brother when Allison was just a teenager. I guess her mother couldn't cope because, at the end of October that same year, she hung herself from the oak tree in their front yard. Allison's little brother was the first to find her. He was too small to get her down, and none of the neighbors intervened because they thought she was an elaborate Halloween decoration. By the time Allison got home, her brother was sitting in the grass with his knees to his chest, rocking back and forth in the shadow of his mother.

He's been in and out of the nut-hut ever since.

I want to take Allison out, maybe down to Cooler's Pub. We'd talk about our respective situations. How, because of her brother, and me with Gramps, we both know what it's like to sacrifice for a loved one. How we'd do anything for them, but sometimes, usually late at night, the thought of that responsibility sits like a weight on our chest, and it's hard to breathe. And even though helping them likely amounts to the one decent thing in our lives, it also fills us with a paralyzing sense of remorse, not to mention crippling debt.

Then, maybe after all of that, we'd share a plate of potato skins.

But I don't. I don't ask Allison out. I'm too shy I guess, or afraid she'll say no. Plus, I think she likes Lonnie.

The ladies from Renaissance Gardens keep me busy all morning. One client talks about her late husband, a tugboat captain, as she rests her head on my chest. She says her hands and fingers have become so thin she's had to move her wedding ring to her thumb, and since then, nothing has felt the same. Another talks about how some of the women at the home cheat at bridge. She insists on being the Big Spoon, and every time she recounts a lost hand, she gives me an angry little squeeze. Someone's grandma, who smells like buttered toast, spends the hour telling me about the time she was propositioned by Spiro Agnew in the elevator of a Baltimore Howard Johnson's.

Things slow down in the afternoon, and Lonnie decides I should use the free time to repaint one of the Snuggle Suites. Lonnie is always finding these weird paint colors that are supposed to have healing properties and evoke some kind of therapeutic something or other. The color he's picked for Suite 3 is called Shantung. Lonnie says it's the shade of the sun just as it rises. He says it's the color of new possibilities, of seeing things in a fresh light. I say it looks yellow to me, and Lonnie says that's exactly my problem. Then he presses some money into my palm and says two gallons ought to cover it.

I decide to take Gramps with me. I find him in the Stillwater Room, on the loveseat with Allison. His head is on her shoulder, and she is holding one of his hands in both of hers. They've got "Rain on a Tin Roof" playing as their Ambient Aural Therapy. I've always liked that one.

Allison must hear me come in, because she looks up and smiles at me. A strand of her chestnut-colored hair falls across her face.

Oh, Allison. When will our time come? When will we—free from having to sweep up the little tumbleweeds of lint and hair that collect under the beds, or having to constantly restock the scented candles because they burn down so quickly, because Lonnie is too cheap to buy the good ones—have our moment? Some time where we can talk, and not just idle chitchat, but about grander, deeper topics. And maybe, during this conversation, one of us, say me, makes a comment that while witty on the surface also speaks to a more profound, emotional understanding of things. And perhaps, in response to this witty/emotional comment, one of us, say you, laughs and gently touches my arm, letting your hand linger for just a second. When will that happen?

Allison catches me staring at her, and her eyes seem to brighten, as if lit from within.

Maybe now, I think. Maybe now is our moment. Then Gramps catches me staring.

"Who the hell is this guy?" he asks.

Maybe not.

"Hi Gramps," I say. "You having a nice time?"

He turns to Allison. "Do you know this young man?" he asks.

Gramps always refers to me as a "young man" when he doesn't recognize me.

"Sure," Allison says. "He's your grandson."

Gramps stares at her, and then me, giving us the same blank look. Prerecorded rain continues to fall.

"I've got some errands to run," I say. "I think you should come with me."

Gramps starts making this low, humming noise and slowly shaking his head.

"I'll take you to lunch," I say.

The humming stops and his posture straightens. "Schotblatt's?" he asks.

That is just great. Gramps doesn't remember me, who he has known my entire life, but he can recall, with immediate clarity, the Reuben from Schotblatt's Deli.

"Sure. Schotblatt's it is," I say, and off we go.

As Gramps and I exit The Shack, the protestors quiet down and step aside, creating a little path. I think, finally, I'm catching a break.

But no. The protestors aren't stepping aside for me. They're making room for the Bald Armoire. He stops a few feet in front of me. He's got a look of concentration on his face that makes the skin around his eyes crinkle.

"Was it you or the other guy that done it?" he says.

"Done what?" I say.

"Killed my mama."

Growing up, mom always said that I had a smart mouth. That I didn't think before I spoke. But, really, it was more like thoughts came out of my mouth the same time they came into my head, and sometimes they bypassed my head entirely. Mom said that one day my smart mouth would get me in trouble.

And she was right. Because instead of apologizing, or explaining what really happened, or offering any measure of sympathy, I say this:

"Holy crap! Mrs. Simone was your mom? I never knew she had a son. In all the time we spent together, she never once mentioned you."

I know, as the words leave my mouth, that this is probably an ill-advised response. The Armoire winces. Then he does this ragged-type breathing through his nose that makes his massive chest rise and fall. Then, as if to confirm my suspicions, he pulls a gun from the waistband of his jean shorts and shoots me.

The Bald Armoire shoots me right in the stomach. I can't believe it. The impact knocks me right on my rear, which, oddly, hurts more than the bullet and fresh hole in my gut.

The gunshot creates a panic. The protestors flee in every direction, their abandoned signs littering the sidewalk. Even The Armoire seems to have disappeared. The peace and quiet is a welcomed change, even if it, I suppose, comes at a hefty price.

I lie back and stare at the sky. There are no clouds.

After some time, I feel my shoulders and head rise, and I think this is it, my body is ascending to that vast and mysterious beyond just like movies and TV always promised. Then I'm disappointed that even death has become a cliché. Then I feel the scratch of polyester against my cheek and realize it's Gramps pulling me into his lap.

"There, there, young man," he says as he gently pats me on the head. "Help will be along soon. Try to lie still."

And even though it hurts my neck, I tilt my head back to look at my grandfather. He looks down at me, and smiles, and continues to stroke my hair.

"You know," he says, "my grandson is taking me to lunch today."

I look away. I close my eyes.

You would think that after so many times of Gramps forgetting who I am, that it wouldn't hurt anymore. But it still does.

It hurts every time.

The Reluctant Son of a Fake Hero

At noon I climb out of the mouth of the Hollywood/Highland metro station just in time to see the 212 bus thunder past, and Frank's cape billow in its wake. He's striking the classic pose—chest out, hands fisted on his hips—and as much as I hate to admit it, he looks pretty good. Considering. He's kept up his physique. He's got actual muscles beneath his suit, unlike most of the losers out here in their Halloween costumes with the drawn-on pecs and the injection-molded abs.

There are few tourists on the boulevard at this time of day, but soon a family of three stops to admire Frank. A series of photos are taken. In one, Frank wraps an arm around the wife while flexing the other so his bicep bulges against the blue fabric of his suit. In another, Frank picks up their daughter, a chubby blonde in pink overalls. He places the girl on his shoulder, squares his jaw, and points a fist to the sky. Then the husband hands Frank some money.

I walk up as they leave.

"A dollar?" Frank says. "I pick up their little piglet and the best they can do is a dollar. Jesus. I gotta start charging by the pound."

Then Frank balls up the money and sticks it in the fanny pack he keeps hidden beneath his cape.

This is my father.

Three days ago, my mom and her new husband had a baby. She and Richard thought that with the chaos of all the visiting relatives, and the needs of the baby, my spending the summer with Frank might be best for everyone.

Everyone but me.

"What am I supposed to do with Frank all summer? What about my friends?" I asked, hoping Mom wouldn't mention the fact that I spend most nights sitting alone on the roof, watching the lights of the city. Watching the horizon of planes waiting to land at LAX. Watching life happen to everyone but me.

"You can always help your father with his latest business venture," Mom said. "That kind of experience will look good on a college application."

It will have to look good. It will have to look magnificent to distract from the school bus fire that is my 2.2 GPA.

"And what is Frank up to nowadays?" I said.

Since their divorce, my father has bounced around from one hairbrained scheme to the next, usually leaving behind a trail of failed businesses and outstanding debts.

Mom winced slightly like she does when trying to think. "Oh, now, what was it he told me? Something about Brand Management and Public Relations."

It turns out that Brand Management and Public Relations means Frank stands on Hollywood Boulevard dressed like Superman and poses for pictures with tourists for tips.

So, yeah, this should be an invaluable experience.

Frank zips up his fanny pack and then stares at me as if I've just materialized there with my suitcase and backpack. As if he hasn't noticed I've been standing beside him for the last thirty seconds, which is probably because he hasn't.

"How was your trip?" he says.

"A bus and a train."

Then Frank asks if I've eaten.

I tell him I could go for some lunch.

So we go to lunch.

We walk down to the Burrito Burro. Frank likes to stay on the boulevard when he's working. He says a lot of the costumed characters do. He says the farther you get away from Hollywood Boulevard, the faster the context and environment break down. Suddenly, you're all alone. Suddenly, you're just some weirdo in an ill-fitting Toys "R" Us costume.

"That's how you get your ass kicked," Frank says. "Even in LA."

The walls of the Burrito Burro are papered with pictures of their mascot. Benny. Benny the Burrito Burro. Alliteration abounds. Benny's a donkey with a burrito for a body: four legs, a head, and a tail sticking out of a tortilla tube. I'm not sure of the advertising intent, but, to me, it suggests that their burritos are made with donkey meat.

I order two tacos.

"So," Frank says in between bites of his burrito, "your mom kicked you out, huh? It's okay. I've been there."

"It's not like that," I say. "Mom's just got more than she can deal with right now."

Frank waves this off. "Your mother likes to think of herself as particular," he says. "I am the proof she is not. Besides, now you're free to join the family business."

"What?" I say.

"You're going to work with me on the boulevard."

"The hell I am."

"You can't just spend the summer sponging off me," he says.

I think: You haven't sent me so much as a birthday card in the last four years.

"I'll get a job," I say.

"Doing what?" Frank says. "Flipping burgers? Cutting some old lady's lawn? What's that gonna pay? Out here, I make upwards of two-hundred a day."

"Really?" I say.

"Cash money. Tax free. We'll work as a team," Frank says. "It'll be good for both of us. Groups always make more than solos."

I stare at my tacos and think about it.

"Plus," Frank says, and a smile breaks across his face, and I know exactly where this is going. "You've got costumed experience."

What a jerk he is.

What a jerk he is to bring that up.

Last year I spent five soul-sucking weeks working for Luxury Souvenirs. I was hired to help promote their $5 Deal Daze. Basically, the plastic crap that usually went for ten dollars was marked down to five. To promote this bonanza of savings, they stuck me outside of the store dressed like Lincoln. They gave me a black wool suit and a top hat. They gave me a stick-on beard that itched my face hours after I peeled it off. They gave me a cardboard sign with a giant five-dollar bill on it.

They also gave me a series of savings-related Lincoln-isms to memorize and recite.

People would walk by, and I'd say, *Emancipate yourself from the slavery of overpriced keepsakes.*

Or, sometimes, I'd remind them that while *A house divided against itself cannot stand, a price tag divided is a heck of a deal.*

Did this sad charade have any impact on the customers? Any increase in revenue? I don't know.

I do know that after eight hours in the sun, in that ridiculous outfit, with sweat pooled in my lower back, and my pride baked down to nothing, I fantasized about someone sneaking up behind me and shooting me in the head.

I think about Frank's offer. The last thing I need is another job standing in public dressed like an idiot. Then I think about two hundred dollars a day for the rest of the summer. That kind of cash could really improve my social standing. I think about junior prom and how the only girl that agreed to go with me was the Snake Mother. That's not her real name. It's Meg. Sophomore year Meg found an egg in the field behind the cafeteria. She decided to keep it warm in her ample cleavage. Meg's sort of a big girl. Then one day, in the middle of Mr. Muzika's Econ lecture, the egg hatched and a snake slithered out. I think about the prom and how, when Meg wasn't looking, the guys from the lacrosse team would flick their tongues at me.

No.

Never again.

I tell Frank I'll do it when a black Spiderman walks in.

Frank waves him over to our table.

"This is my kid," he says. "And this is Bugatti."

"Like the car," Bugatti says as we shake hands.

"Nice to meet you, Bugatti."

"Like the car," he says again.

"Nice to meet you, Bugatti like the car."

Then Bugatti says, "Check it out," while swinging his leg wide and dropping his foot on the middle of our table.

I slide my tacos closer.

He's wearing red high-top sneakers with black webbing on them. "Specially made," he says.

"Why not just wear the shoes that came with the costume?" I say.

"No good," Bugatti says. "Spidey boots got no ankle support."

Frank tells Bugatti about my decision to join him on the boulevard. He tells him that we're trying to figure out my costume.

"What about Captain America?" I say.

"Bad idea," Frank says. "There's already too many. You can't swing a dead cat down here without hitting a Captain America."

Bugatti nods in agreement.

"Plus," Frank says, "it's bad business to combine the universes."

"Pardon me?" I say.

Frank goes on to explain that Captain America is from the Marvel universe while Superman is from the DC universe.

"You don't blend them," he says. "It ruins credibility."

"That's what bursts the bubble?" I say. "That the fake people aren't from the same fake place? That, and not the fact that Mexican Spider-man is like fifty pounds overweight?"

Bugatti slams his fist on the table.

One of my tacos falls over.

"I hate that motherfucker," he says.

"It may be stupid," Frank says, "but it matters to the people. That's the business. If you and I are going to work together, you gotta be DC."

"Okay, fine," I say, leaning back in my chair. "I'll be Batman."

Bugatti groans at me, shakes his head side to side.

"No good," Frank says. "It's the cowl. You want to avoid cowls and masks like they're an STD. Otherwise, come August, you'll be drowning in your own sweat."

I think back to the Lincoln beard.

"It's true," Bugatti says, holding up his Spiderman mask. "And I've got a high heat tolerance."

In the end, somehow, we settle on Aquaman. Frank says I've already got the blonde hair. He says my lanky and somewhat girlish physique won't be a problem, as Aquaman isn't really known for his muscles.

That stings a bit.

Frank says I'll be the only one on the boulevard. He says, combined with his Superman, we'll be a moneymaking powerhouse.

I agree.

I agree and become Aquaman.

With Aquaman, I have a few options, stylistically speaking. There's the purple and blue camouflage outfit from the 1973 *Aquaman Adventures* television series starring Bruce Hortnutt. Unfortunately, that show was short lived. Turns out, Hortnutt was something of a bunny hoarder. His neighbors complained about the smell for months. By the time Animal Protective Services kicked down the door, there were over a thousand of them, bunnies reproducing as they do. They said the backyard, which was nothing more than a fenced-in field, was filled with them. They said it was pink eyes and floppy ears as far as you could see. That you couldn't spot a blade of grass. They said it was like some alternate universe where the Earth was made of bunnies.

When the news went public, Hortnutt hung himself.

So, I'm probably not going with that look.

There's also the rough and tumble look from Aquaman's edgy rebranding attempt in the mid-nineties. In this version, he has a golden harpoon attached to his left arm to replace the hand he lost in a piranha attack, which is pretty badass. But he's also shirtless, and sports long hair, and a wild, unkempt beard. I'm not sure I can stand shirtless in the middle of Hollywood Boulevard. People would confuse me with an emaciated hobo. Plus, I promised myself I was finished with stick-on beards.

Ultimately, I decide to go with the classic look.

On the walk back from the Burrito Burro, Frank says he has some emerald tights and gloves from a brief stint as the Green Lantern. He says the black trunks will be easy to find. For Aquaman's famous orange and gold-scaled shirt, Frank says he has an old wetsuit top I can use.

"It's not gonna be perfect," he says as we reach the metro station, "but you'll still look better than half of these clowns. And you'll have the advantage of standing beside me."

Then he reaches into his fanny pack and pulls out some keys. He says his apartment is off Sunset, just a few blocks past Fairfax. He says he'll see me later.

"Wait," I say. "You're not going to drive me?"

"No."

"That's like five miles from here. Why not?"

Frank sighs. Then he raises his palm, and makes a slow sweep of the boulevard, from the Baby Gap all the way down to the Hollywood Museum of Squandered Innocence.

"I'm at work," he says.

I decide to walk. I decide that my forgoing the bus and lugging my belongings down Sunset Boulevard will somehow punish Frank. That he will see the error of his ways and pull up alongside me, apologize for being selfish, ask for forgiveness.

This is delusional. Frank has always only cared about himself.

For probably the last year of their marriage, Mom suspected he was cheating on her. Then, one day, her suspicions were confirmed when she found gum in his pubic hair. I heard them fighting through my bedroom wall. I heard Frank's futile attempts to convince Mom the gum was his. How it must have fallen out of his mouth and become stuck there.

"Like, maybe, when I was in the shower," he said.

There was more, but I piled the pillows over my head. I didn't want to hear. The next morning, Frank was gone. Mom said he'd be away for a while, out of town on business. She said it to spare me the pain I guess. I guess she assumed I hadn't heard them fighting. As with Frank, as with a lot of things in life, Mom gave the thickness of our walls more credit than they deserved.

A few days later, I saw Frank on the high school baseball field. He was drunk and making languid loops in the outfield on a girl's bicycle. He'd been sleeping in the dugout.

Frank's apartment building is one of those white stucco jobs that crumble into pebbles and powder when touched. He's got a ground floor apartment, the one closest to the road. Inside, it's just one giant room. There's a weight bench in one corner with a pair of underwear hanging off one end of the barbell. Dumbbells of various sizes and weight litter the floor. I watch my step. I head to the galley kitchen hoping for a glass of water. Tubs of protein powder and beer cans crowd the counter. Frank has exactly one glass, and there's a cigarette butt floating in it, and lipstick on the rim. I drop my pack and flop down on Frank's bed. On his nightstand are a copy of *The Entrepreneur in You* and a framed photo of Christopher Reeve, the actor who starred in the original *Superman* movies. There's not a picture of me in sight.

I think about calling my mom. I think if I explain the situation, Frank's ridiculous "job" and the squalor of his apartment, then she'll let me come home. Then I think she'd just as likely tell me to give it some time. To give Frank a chance and make the best of it.

I close my eyes.

The drone of the traffic is familiar and soothing.

I wake up to Frank kicking my foot. He's shirtless, and wearing clear plastic gloves that are streaked with black.

"Are you dyeing your hair?" I say.

"You bet your ass I am."

"Why?"

"Because you can't have a graying Superman."

"Why?"

"For the same reason Jesus died in his prime. Nobody wants to see their heroes age. It reminds them of their own mortality."

Then he waves a gloved hand at his bed and me. "I hope you enjoyed your little nap," he says. "But don't make a habit of it." He points to a sagging, purple loveseat whose integrity looks suspect. "That's you," he says.

"Excuse me?"

"It doesn't look like much, but it's pretty comfortable," Frank says. "And it pulls out, which makes it smarter than me." Then Frank lets out a single burst of laughter and kicks me again. He peels the gloves off with his teeth and picks up a white linen shirt from the floor. On the back of the shirt is a hula dancer with a pair of monstrous breasts crammed into a coconut bra. She has a grass skirt made of green fringe that sways back and forth when Frank moves. She is naked underneath and rendered anatomically correct. The level of detail is alarming.

"This stuff needs fifteen minutes to set in and do its thing," Frank says walking to the fridge. He tosses me a beer. "While we wait, let's go on the roof," he says. "It's a good place to drink, but then again most places are."

So we go to the roof.

We make our way across the tarpaper, past all of the satellite TV dishes, to the far corner. From here I can see the traffic crawling along Sunset Boulevard. I can see how the brake lights waver in the exhaust.

Across the street, and above the Chinese Food & Donuts place, is a billboard. They are, apparently, remaking *Citizen Kane*. The billboard features the bloated face of the Scottish actor who will play Kane. He used to be leaner, and more of a star, but lately he's only made headlines for throwing people through barroom windows and becoming a casual anti-Semite.

Frank sees the billboard, too. "Can you believe they're rehashing that garbage?" he says.

No, I think, I can't. Who needs another movie about someone desperate to relive his childhood? Another movie that glorifies that time instead of depicting it for the parade of regret and loneliness that it really is.

It's surprising to find myself agreeing with Frank. Surprising, but nice.

"I mean," he says, "when is Hollywood gonna stop pushing their homoerotic agenda?"

"Wait. What?"

"That movie's about gay sex."

"How do you figure?"

Frank holds up his hand. He curls his index finger along his thumb.

"I don't know what that means," I say.

"It's an asshole."

"And?"

"Rosebud is slang for 'asshole,'" Frank says. "The guy spends the entire movie looking for his rosebud. He's trying to relive his first homosexual experience. The movie's about gay sex."

"It's not," I say. "It's about a sad, rich guy pining for his childhood. Rosebud was the name of his sled."

"Believe what you want, but you're wrong. Plus," Frank says, "'Charles Foster Kane?' That's one of the biggest puffer names I've ever heard." Then Frank belches and turns his back on me, concluding one of our better father-son talks.

Some nights I lie awake, thinking about how half of my genetic makeup comes from this guy. Then I think about the traits I got from Mom, and I wonder if they're good enough, strong enough, to counteract Frank's contaminated contribution.

A gust of wind comes in from the west. It blows the hula dancer's skirt to the side, and I try not to stare.

I try and I fail.

The next morning, we go to work.

Frank insists on being on the boulevard no later than nine a.m. Any later than that, he says, and all of the quality real estate is taken. So, at 8:58, we're standing at the base of the stairs leading to the Hollywood & Highland Shopping Center.

"This way," he tells me, "we'll get all of the shopper traffic, and all of the boulevard traffic."

It sounds smart. It sounds smart until the first hour ticks by without anyone wanting a picture. No one wants a picture the next hour, or the hour after that. The only highlight of the morning is when a woman walks by with a rattlesnake tattooed on her legs. She has the snake's head on her left calf, and its body going up the back of her leg until it disappears beneath her black leather skirt. The rest of its body continues down her other thigh, with the rattler on her right calf.

"Will you look at that," Frank says. "I'll bet the rest of that thing—" and he pauses, sticks up a finger, makes little circles, "—is coiled on her ass. Just imagine that." Then Frank digs a small notebook out of his fanny pack and writes something down.

"What are you doing?" I say.

"I don't want to lose that," he says. "That's some beautiful imagery. It'll work great in one of my poems."

"Your what?"

"My poems. My poetry. I write poems from time to time," he says.

This is a curious development. Frank never struck me as the literary type. He used to read *Sports Illustrated* on the toilet, occupying our sole bathroom for up to an hour, but that was about it.

"I'd like to read something sometime," I say.

"Yeah, maybe," he says.

Then we go to lunch.

When we get back, the spot by the stairs is filled with sunshine, so we move down the boulevard and stand in the shade of the double-decker Star Sightings tour bus.

No one wants a picture.

"Let's try splitting up," Frank says. "If one of us gets a nibble, he'll wave over the other one. We'll divide and conquer."

"Frank," I say, "this is stupid. I feel stupid."

"Hey, if it was easy, anyone would be doing it. You gotta get out there and generate interest. Try using that thing you made."

The night before, Frank told me I should add a prop to my costume. Something for tourists to pose with. Something to help draw them in.

"Zorro's got a sword," he said. "Thor has a hammer. All the lesser heroes do it."

I didn't appreciate being referred to as a "lesser hero," but then I pictured myself in green tights and an orange neoprene shirt, and I figured I could use all of the help I could get. I spent the night taping paper towel tubes together and covering the whole thing in aluminum foil.

It's supposed to be a trident.

It looks like a big, limp fork.

Another hour goes by. No one wants my picture. Then I see Frank pose with a young couple. A few minutes later, he takes a picture with a group of girls in matching softball uniforms.

I storm down the street. "What the hell?"

"What?" Frank says.

"You said you'd wave me over."

"I tried," Frank says. "They didn't want their picture with you. They thought you were some kind of Dutch farm boy."

I feel my face bloom hot with embarrassment.

I toss the trident.

I spend the rest of the afternoon across the street, sulking inside The Dripping Bean and nursing a black coffee.

Around three, Frank comes by. He says he's going to a Happy Hour with Bugatti and a couple of guys who dress as Iron Man. I ask if I can come.

"You can if you've got any money," he says.

I go back to Frank's. This time I take the bus.

By ten o'clock, Frank hasn't come home, so I steal two of his beers and go to the roof. There are never many visible stars in LA's night sky, but down here, it's even worse. The streetlights and spotlights and digital billboards and winking neon are too much for even the brightest of celestial bodies. The light pollution reflects off of the smog, making a gray blanket of the sky. It's easy to imagine that this is all there is. That nothing larger or grander exists beyond this tiny bubble. It's easy to imagine that we are all alone.

I walk to the edge of the roof. I have never looked over a roof I haven't imagined myself jumping off of. Sometimes, I imagine the things that would cycle through my head on the way down. If there would be some clarity before I hit, and if it's better to experience that and have it immediately taken away than never to have any at all.

On the other side of Frank's building is an alley. The far wall is lined with dumpsters, and on every single one is a sign that reads, NO

BABIES.

The next morning, Frank wakes me with a coffee and a blueberry scone. I don't know if this is his way for apologizing for yesterday, but I'll take it.

When we get to the boulevard, he hands me a folded piece of paper. I open it and see that it is titled: The Sex With You.

"What the hell is this? I say.

"My words," he says.

"What?"

"You said you wanted to read some of my stuff," Frank says. "This is one of my poems."

"Oh, okay," I say. "Sure."

I read Frank's poem.

The sex with you
It has been terrible for years.
Your vagina has become
nothing more than a
hole.
A grave
where I bury
the best part
of myself.

"That's something," I say, handing the paper back to Frank. "Very evocative."

"I wrote it about your mother," he says.

"Jesus Christ! What the hell is your problem, Frank?"

"You know," he says, "you should try calling me Dad."

"Please," I say. "I'd sooner call you Superman."

The rest of the morning is awkward. A few people stop for pictures, but they only want Frank. Sometimes I get thrown in at the end, as an afterthought, but mostly I just work the camera.

Then an Asian grandmother, with a group of kids in tow, gets my hopes up. As her grandchildren gather around Frank, flexing their little muscles, she pushes her camera into my chest.

"Pictureman," she says, smiling.

"No," I say. "Aquaman. I'm a hero, too."

"Pictureman," she says again, frowning, and pressing the camera harder. Then she joins her grandchildren, everyone posing and smiling for a picture.

So I take their picture.

She hands Frank some money before they continue down the boulevard.

"Don't worry Pictureman," Frank says. "You'll get your cut."

"This is stupid," I say. "It isn't working. I can't do this."

"Sure you can," Frank says, putting a hand on my shoulder.

"No," I say, sliding away from his touch. "I can't. I'm not like you." And as the words leave my mouth, I realize that it's true. I'm not like Frank, and that, somehow, is part of my problem.

"So, what then?" Frank says. "You want to quit? You want to go home?"

"Yes!" That's exactly what I want. Maybe if I possessed Frank's charm, or strength, or whatever it is that gives him a natural ease with people, then things would be different. But I don't. Maybe if I did, I wouldn't be cast out of my own home, supplanted by a baby my mother barely knows. Maybe I wouldn't be equally embarrassed and grateful to have the Snake Mother as a prom date. Maybe I wouldn't spend every night on the roof, alone, wishing for things to be different and having no idea what that difference looks like.

Frank just stands there and furrows his brow. It makes his Superman curl, the one he molds each morning then lacquers with hairspray, move ever so slightly. "What did you say?"

"I said I'll stay," I mumble, not meeting his eyes. Then I shuffle to the center of the boulevard, positioning myself between the streams of tourist traffic. "I'll try."

And I do. I make eye contact. I wave. I stretch my face into an unnatural smile and project a confidence I do not own. I make a true and unguarded attempt to engage.

No one wants my picture.

Endangered Animal Release Specialists

Monday morning, I hurry to the Intake & Assignment meeting and tell myself this time things will be different. This time my potential and experience will be recognized. This time I will be assigned a high-profile case. Do I think it will be a Tibetan antelope or a Mediterranean monk seal? Of course not, though a girl can dream. Still, after months of releasing amphibians, really anything from the class Mammalia would feel like a bonus. I just need something to be proud of. Something that will let me feel the work I'm doing here is making a difference. Something I can counter with when Ma cruelly, and inaccurately, asks why I'm wasting my life as an animal masturbator.

I arrive just as everyone is taking their seats and Dr. Farragut is plugging in the projector. When we're settled and everyone has helped themselves to coffee and a doughnut, Dr. Farragut begins the meeting. He begins the same way he has every Monday morning for the last six months.

"How are you, you bunch of jag-offs?"

It's his favorite joke. He, still, thinks it's hilarious. We offer a pained smile or an obligatory half-laugh in response. All of us except Janet.

The fire, and subsequent scarring and muscle deterioration, has rendered Janet's face incapable of any real expression. Dr. Farragut says the shiny pink scar tissue makes her face look like a glazed ham, which, while somewhat accurate, isn't very nice. Either way, no one expects Janet to pretend to be happy.

I envy her.

Then the lights go dark, and the meeting really begins. Our first Intake slide features a long, ashen face ringed in copper-colored fur. Everyone perks up. *Pongo abelii,* or, as he is more commonly known, the Sumatran orangutan, is listed as Critically Endangered. Less than 7,000 remain. This is an extremely high-profile case. Lots of potential press. Lots of potential notoriety.

"I know what you're all thinking," Dr. Farragut says. "*Pongo abelii* is a high-profile case that will garner a great deal of attention. As such, I think it's best if I personally handle the release of this animal."

No one is surprised. Dr. Farragut always assigns himself the most noteworthy cases. In his office is a framed copy of *Conservation Quarterly.* Dr. Farragut is on the cover with Ozzie, the Brazilian ocelot he assigned to himself and released to much fanfare. The article is titled, "The Man, and the Hands, That Have the Ocelot on the Rise." Dr. Farragut had Ozzie autograph the cover by dipping his paws in ink, which, to me, seems tacky.

It's not as if I'm not happy for the ocelots. I am. They're beautiful creatures. But it's hard to forget that the day the reporters came, and took their pictures, and made a big show of everything, I was down in the sub-basement trying to release an extremely uncooperative poison dart frog.

But still, through it all, I bide my time and quietly endure.

The next slide shows a familiar face. Duncan is a four-year-old spectacled bear on Temporary Transfer from the Scranton facility.

Dr. Farragut tells us that Duncan has recently been classified as a Problem Specimen because he attacked his Release Specialist. He tells us this as if we all haven't watched the security footage about a million times.

At first things seemed to be going well. The Release Specialist began with some lower-abdominal massage. Duncan looked content. Soon, he achieved complete rigidity. The Specialist appeared to have a firm, but not too firm grip, and a steady, even rhythm.

That's textbook technique.

But then something went wrong. It wasn't clear what. Maybe the Specialist got lazy. Or over-confident. Maybe he looked the animal in the eye, which is completely verboten.

That's the first thing we learn in Orientation.

Regardless, Duncan leapt from the Release Bay, landed on the Specialist, and pinned him to the floor. A muffled whimper could be heard on the audio. Duncan inflicted some minor lacerations to the chest and neck area, and chewed off the tip of an ear before the boys from Control swarmed in with their tranq guns.

Dr. Farragut reminds us about Duncan's temperament. He warns us to be cautious. Then he assigns Duncan to Janet. I look over to see if Janet is excited, or nervous, about being given such a challenging animal, but of course I can't tell.

I'm next to get an assignment. I close my eyes and hope for a black-footed ferret or an African wild dog. I hear the click of the projector. Then I hear Monroe snort out a laugh. I don't even know what Monroe is doing here. He's not a Release Specialist. He runs the Cryogenics Lab. But still, he's here every Monday morning, inhaling the free doughnuts and then sucking the jelly and powdered-sugar from his fingers in a suggestive manner.

I open my eyes. I see a mosaic of black, brown, and yellow pebbled skin. I see two marbled golden eyes and the distinctive upturned snout that rests between them. Great. The Puerto Rican crested toad. Another amphibian.

I begin to protest, but Dr. Farragut raises a hand, silencing me.

"Before you start in with the lack of variety in your Release Assignments, or how you feel underappreciated, or how I must have some personal vendetta against you, let me assure you, I do not. Would I love to assign you a pygmy hippopotamus or an African bush elephant? Of course I would. But do you see any African bush elephants around here? Because I don't."

Then Dr. Farragut makes a show of looking around the room, and under the table, as if he has simply misplaced an African bush elephant. Which is ridiculous. They're huge.

"I can only assign what we intake," he says.

I think about mentioning the orangutan, but I don't.

"Plus," Dr. Farragut continues, "would you prefer Duncan? Would you prefer the bear that may claw your pretty little face off? Not that I believe that will happen. Not for a second. But it might. And as such, I have to try to minimize risk. I have to try to minimize the collateral damage in a before-and-after type of assessment. Am I making myself clear?"

Janet and I stare blankly ahead.

Monroe devours another doughnut.

Then Dr. Farragut sighs and runs a hand over his hair. Not through. Just over. Dr. Farragut is extremely meticulous about his hair. Every light-brown strand is slicked back into a smooth dome. It reminds me of the shell of the Yangtze giant turtle.

Which is also endangered.

Which is also another animal I'll probably never get my hands on.

"Okay," Dr. Farragut says. "Let's say it's raining. It's raining and I have the option between a work boot and a fancy shoe. Maybe the work boot is scuffed up a bit. Maybe the leather's cracked, and the sole is loose. You get the idea. The point is, with this particular kind of weather, there's a chance of some destructive, and overall disastrous impact befalling one of my shoes. Again, for the record, I believe that said danger is unlikely. But the potential is there. Puddles and mud and whatnot. And so, should some damage occur, it will be less noticeable on the shoe with the aforementioned wear and tear: the work boot. So Janet gets the bear, and you get the toad, and I have an early lunch."

Then Dr. Farragut slaps the table, stands, and exits the meeting.

I turn to Janet. I wish there was some indication of how she's feeling. She's taking long, audible breaths through what's left of her nose, so it's probably not good.

"Janet," I say, "I'm so sorry. I should have never said anything."

"Unbelievable," she says, standing up so fast her chair rolls back into the plastic ficus. "If anyone in this glorified animal bath house is a fancy shoe, it's me." Then she spins on her heel and storms out of the room.

I spend the rest of the morning looking for Janet. I look in each of the Collection Centers. I look in Processing and Analysis. I check Animal Enclosures and watch Duncan destroy a perfectly good tire swing. I check the Cafeteria, and though I don't find Janet, I realize I could have some lunch. So I have some lunch.

I get in line and am immediately flanked by Rod and Derek, two stooges from Insemination. Rod has porcelain veneers that are an unnatural, glaring shade of white. Derek has a way of working his beach house in Montauk into every conversation. Both think they're better than everyone in Release. Most of Insemination does. In a way they're probably right. People tend to only care about the aftereffect, the final result. They fixate on the fruit, or the flower, and rarely give a thought to the seeds that make them possible.

Still, it doesn't help that Rod and Derek are insufferable morons.

"So," Rod says, leaning over as I try to help myself to some salad, "I heard things didn't go so well at Intake and Assignment."

"More amphibians?" Derek says. "Poor girl."

"You know," Rod says, "since you've become such an expert at releasing amphibians, maybe you could help me out. I've got a trouser snake that could use a release." Then he smiles, and my pupils dilate.

"Or, if you're afraid of snakes," Derek says, "I've got a crotch lizard you may be interested in. I could show it to you this weekend. I just put in a hot tub at the Montauk house."

Then they both laugh and high-five over my head.

I feel like reminding them that snakes and lizards are reptiles, not amphibians, but I don't. It's a sad and pathetic defense. Instead I carry my tray to the corner table and sit facing the wall and eat my stupid lunch.

Things weren't always like this. I used to be a vet. I used to have a job I loved, and kind, supportive co-workers. Then, one day, all of that was taken away. My then boyfriend, current ex-boyfriend, current pile of human garbage, had been stealing my keys to the clinic and proximity card to the narcotics locker. Apparently, he'd been doing it for the better part of a year. At first, it was just a few pills here and there. But later, as his addiction grew, he was stealing entire bottles. He replaced the missing pills with Tic Tacs, never stopping to think that, at some point, someone might notice the Canine Oxycodone smelled like Arctic Peppermint.

What an idiot he was.

What an idiot I am.

When the police showed up with a search warrant they found over $3,000 worth of pills in his tennis bag. Which now makes sense since I never once saw him play tennis. He folded right there, went full hysterical. Between wet, stuttering breaths, he copped to everything. Stealing the card. Stealing the drugs. Then he also admitted that he'd been cheating on me with a girl who was addicted to horse enemas.

The entire time he's leaking tears and snot on my good rug.

Though I was cleared on all charges, my reputation, my practice, were destroyed.

Sometimes, late at night, I lie in bed and wonder what my problem is. Why I allowed myself to lose everything to a guy who, I knew, deep down, wasn't good for me. I wouldn't say I saw a future with him, though, at the time, I like to believe I did, if only to justify the years I wasted. I like to think of myself as an intelligent person, but, sometimes, I just don't know. I do know that because of my latest lapse in judgment I am no longer a veterinarian. I am now here, surrounded by frogs and toads, all of us, in our own way, struggling to exist.

I finally find Janet in the Allen Lindstrom Memorial Break Room. Dr. Lindstrom is credited as single-handedly moving the Iberian lynx from the Critically Endangered to Endangered category on the IUCN Red List.

Single-handedly. That's one of our little jokes. Because, as everyone knows, releasing an Iberian lynx is, at least, a two-handed job.

"Mind if I sit?" I say, and Janet nods to one of the chairs. "I think I owe you an apology."

"No," she says, "you don't. The whole thing was ridiculous. Who screams 'I'm a fancy shoe' at work?"

"Dr. Farragut knows how to push people. He was out of line," I say.

"His entire being begs for tolerance."

"Yeah," I say. "That, too."

Just then Dr. Farragut walks in. "What's all this?" he says.

"We were just talking about work," I say. "Our latest assignments."

"Oh?" he says as he takes a seat next to Janet. "You don't mind if I smoke, do you?" Then he leans unnecessarily close to Janet as he lights his cigarette. Her entire body stiffens at the sight of the flame.

Things have been tense between Dr. Farragut and Janet ever since Dr. Farragut learned that Janet and his ex-wife were seeing each other.

"You're not afraid of a little bear are you?" Dr. Farragut says. "Tough gal like yourself?"

Janet stares at the floor for a second and then looks fully at Dr. Farragut. "Every day I see the way people look at me," she says. "The way they stare when they're trying to hide the fact that they're staring. I hear what people say when they think they're far enough away. When they think they're being quiet. So no, I'm not worried about that bear hurting me."

"That's fascinating," Dr. Farragut says. "Good for you. You know what I'd like to see and hear? You getting back to work. We're on a deadline, and that bear isn't going to juice himself."

When I get back to my office, there is a message from Ma telling me to hurry home because it's her turn to host the Yellow Hat Society meeting. Then, there is another message asking me to stop and pick up some almond milk because a few of the Yellow Hat ladies are lactose intolerant. Then there is a third message telling me to make sure that the almond milk is unsweetened, because some of the ladies that are lactose intolerant are also diabetic.

Ma moved in after I lost my veterinary practice. Not out of support. Nothing like that. She moved in when she got evicted from Horizons, her eldercare facility. I didn't even know they could do that. Evict people. But they can. They did.

They called me at work. They said there'd been an incident. That was the word the woman on the phone used. *Incident*. I pressed for specifics, but she was unwilling. When I arrived, I found a stern-looking nurse standing behind the Admin desk and Ma sitting off to the side with her suitcases stacked around her.

"What seems to be the problem?" I said.

"There was minor disagreement about the allocation of desserts which, unfortunately, evolved into an eviction-worthy event."

"I don't know what that means."

"It means they screwed me out of my cake!" Ma screamed.

The nurse glared at me and then continued. "Each night we deliver a fully prepared dinner to our residents. This meal, barring any specific dietary restrictions, includes a dessert. Last night's dessert was a piece of German chocolate cake."

"Okay," I said.

"Your mother claims that she never received her piece of cake."

"Because I didn't!" Ma screamed again.

"I'm sorry," I said. "Please go on."

"We explained to your mother that each meal is plated in our kitchen, and then that meal is cross-referenced by Distribution. This ensures that every resident receives the correct meal, including dessert. Still, your mother insisted she did not receive her piece of cake."

Ma's been stubborn for as long as I can remember. When I was nine, she tried to sue the Post Office because she was convinced the mailman was using our letters to pick his teeth. For almost a year, she carefully inspected each envelope for any signs of oral defilement.

"The disagreement continued until this morning," the nurse said, "when your mother removed her colostomy bag and dumped its contents in the middle of the TV room, ruining the good recliner."

I looked over at Ma, but she wouldn't meet my eyes. She busied herself picking invisible lint from her slacks.

"Your mother then pointed to the mess and asked us—" and here the nurse paused to read from a clipboard— "'if it looked like there was any fucking cake in there.'"

"Well, did it?" Ma screamed.

I tried to plead my case. I tried to explain the level of care Ma requires, and the number of hours I work, but it didn't make a difference. They cited their inability to continue to tolerate such toxic behavior. They said Ma had to go.

So I took her home.

We stopped at the Food Farm, and I got some things for dinner.

I made up the spare room.

We ate and watched a documentary about Eleanor Roosevelt.

We had cake for dessert.

When I get home, I find a bunch of strange cars in my driveway and the ladies of the Yellow Hat Society gathered in my living room. On paper, the Yellow Hat Society prepares and sends Care Packages to the troops, but what they mainly do is gossip about other members of the neighborhood. That, and snack on easily chewable food.

I once asked Ma if all of the ladies wore yellow hats to their get-togethers. She looked at me with a mixture of disgust and disbelief.

"No," she said. "What kind of stupid question is that?"

Tonight, the Yellow Hats are gossiping about Mrs. Edna Peagrim, and why, after living in the neighborhood for twenty-eight years, including the six since Morris died, she is suddenly moving to Fort Wayne. What terrible tragedy is forcing Mrs. Peagrim to spontaneously flee from what is, really, her one and only home? One of the Yellow Hats suspects early onset dementia. Another assumes cancer.

"A bone or a brain, you know, one of the inoperable kinds."

"They never had kids?" one of the ladies asks.

"No," says another.

"I heard she had one of those barren uteruses," says a third.

"How could she leave?" Ma says. "At this point, we're the only family she has left."

"Then God help her," I say.

Ma shoots me her stink face. The one where she narrows her eyes and sucks in her cheeks. "And what about you?" she asks. "Any chance of you giving me some grandkids before I'm dead in the ground?" Then, to the rest of the group, she says that I scare men.

"My Carissa has that," says one of the Yellow Hats.

"It's that job of hers," Ma says. "I've told her a thousand times that she'll never get a good man when she spends her days surrounded by animal penises."

One of the Yellow Hat ladies puts down her egg salad sandwich and quickly makes the sign of the cross.

I leave them to their philanthropy and head upstairs.

I hate to admit it, but Ma's right. Guys are intimidated by my job. The majority of my first dates are like conversational ticking time bombs. We sit there and talk about where we grew up, our childhood pets, our favorite books.

Tick. Tick. Tick.

Then comes the question about what I do for a living, and, *BOOM*, any chance of me not dying alone is blown to smithereens.

Even the guys who persevere and make it beyond the first few dates eventually develop a sad, and woefully misguided, case of A.P.I.C. Animal Penis Inferiority Complex. It's, apparently, an occupational hazard. As if there aren't enough already. As if releasing a western low-land gorilla is just a stroll through the daisies.

What can I do? I've tried being honest. They say it's the best policy, but, lately, I'm not sure who *they* are, and, more and more, I seriously doubt if *they've* ever tried maintaining a relationship in this sordid day and age.

But still, I've tried being honest. *Yes*, I've told them, *a northern black rhino is bigger than you. Because every part of him is bigger than you. Because he's a goddamn rhinoceros!*

But, by then, I've already lost them.

About an hour later, I hear the Yellow Hat ladies drive away. Then I hear Ma call me from the bathroom.

"Get in here and help an old lady out," she says.

Sometimes Ma needs help reattaching her colostomy bag to her stoma. Which isn't always easy. Ma can be a difficult patient.

"Careful, careful" she says, before I've even touched her. "How about you wash your hands first?"

"My hands are clean," I say.

"Are they? Because your father, God rest his soul, was the only man I let into my bloomers, and I won't have that purity sullied now by your filthy, wooly mammoth penis hands."

"Jesus, Ma. First of all, I wear gloves at work. You know that. And secondly, the wooly mammoth is extinct."

"Oh?" she says. "So you're not good at your job either?"

The next day is Tuesday, which is the day I push the Collection Cart around the facility. I collect any extra samples from Release, and any leftover samples from Insemination, and bring them to Cryogenics to freeze for later use.

When I get there Monroe holds out one hand, stopping me, and shields his eyes with the other. "Don't tell me. Don't tell me," he says.

Monroe fancies himself something of a semen sommelier. He believes he can ascertain the species of any animal just by studying the samples from its release. He's turned this belief into some sort of obscene guessing game. He's never once been right.

Monroe picks up an Extraction Container, making sure to cover the label with his thumb. He swirls it around. He holds it up to the light. Then he unscrews the lid and waves the container under his nose. He inhales deeply.

The day he takes a sip is the day I quit. I've promised myself.

"Ganges river dolphin?" he says.

"Goodbye, Monroe."

"No?" He gives it another swirl. Another sniff. "Southern rockhopper penguin. It's a rockhopper penguin, isn't it?"

I turn to leave.

"C'mon, don't be like that," Monroe says. "Give me a hint. Is it at least a member of Aves class?"

I can still hear him screaming guesses halfway back to my office.

Sometimes I really hate it here

In my office, I find Dr. Farragut sitting on the corner of my desk. He's looking at a picture of Ma and me at the Paul Anka show and making a scrunched-up face.

"Can I help you?"

He puts down the picture. "Follow me," he says.

I follow Dr. Farragut back to his office, and he tells me to take a seat.

"I know you're unsatisfied here," he says. "Frustrated. And who wouldn't be? What with week after week of frogs and toads? Toads and frogs. What with everyone referring to you as the Amphibian Milk Maid? Oh. Were you not aware of that? Doesn't matter. That's in the past. Or, it can be, but first we have to make some changes. Are you ready for that? Are you ready to address what, as I see it, is our supply and demand problem? Because, to me, we have too much demand. And what is demand as it applies to our situation? Is it people? Personnel? It is. We have too many employees, and not enough quality assignments, and what does that give us? Does it give us a nice, qualified person wasting her time, wasting her talent, releasing fringe-limbed tree frogs all day? I think we both know it does. And so, I'd like to propose that we lessen our demand. I'm talking about removing some dead weight. Some over-cooked, hard-to-look at, wife-stealing weight."

I think he's referring to Janet.

"I'm referring to Janet," he says.

"You're going to fire Janet?"

"No," Dr. Farragut says. "Of course not. Not that I wouldn't like to. I'd love to. But I can't. I can't fire her, not with all of the—" Dr. Farragut stops and limply waves a hand around his face, "—you know, that whole mess. That, plus her sexual orientation, which apparently gives her some sort of protected minority status. It basically makes her unfireable. Nope. I'd catch less hell trying to fire Jesus Himself."

"I'm not sure I understand," I say.

Dr. Farragut says that we need a scenario that takes the firing of Janet out of his hands. That puts it above his pay grade. He says we need something that will force her out.

"It's some unpleasant business I know," Dr. Farragut says, "but what else can we do? Do you see any alternatives, because I don't? Perhaps, instead, we should focus on the positive aspects. Because, to me, we both win. You get a higher quality of assignments, which improves morale and makes for a happier workplace. And I no longer have a daily reminder that I've been cuckolded. That I'm a cuckold. Is it cuckold or cuckolded? Doesn't matter."

Then Dr. Farragut says with Janet gone, there's some potential wiggle room in Payroll. He says he'd be willing to talk to Head Office about getting me a promotion.

"How does that sound, Ms. Assistant Director of Facility Operations?"

A promotion? A promotion would be nice. I think about who this would help. I'd be able to hire someone to look after Ma. Maybe, down the road, get us a bigger place. And me. It would help me. I'd outrank Rod and Derek, which should finally shut their moronic mouths. Plus, AD of Facility Ops is a job title that may not ignite the insecurity of every eligible man.

I think about who this would hurt. Janet, of course. It definitely hurts Janet.

Janet used to be a vet, too. She had a nice little practice in Oyster Bay—nothing too stressful, just a bunch of rich old ladies and their tiny, fluff-ball dogs. One morning, a woman came rushing in, screaming and wailing and clutching Biscuits to her chest.

Biscuits is her Pekingese.

Biscuits wasn't breathing. His little heart had stopped. Janet tried oxygen. She tried an IV to maintain blood pressure. She tried chest compressions.

Nothing worked.

Then the woman took out her checkbook. She said she'd give Janet $10,000 if she saved her baby.

So Janet tried one more thing. She tried to shock Biscuits' heart back into action with a defibrillator.

"I don't know what the hell I was thinking," Janet told me. "That dog wasn't much bigger than the paddles."

Janet charged up the machine, shouted *clear*, and administered the first shock.

Nothing.

Then she tried another shock.

It worked. Sort of.

Biscuits sprang back to life, but the electric pulse also set his fur on fire. He leapt from the table and ran around the operating theater.

Janet and her nurse ran after him. The curtains caught fire. The smoke alarm went off.

"I finally got him cornered," Janet said. "I wrapped him up in my lab coat and smothered the flames. But the sleeve of my shirt must have caught fire. At the time, I was going through something of an experimental phase with my wardrobe. My shirt was this shimmery, polyester monstrosity. The thing went up like it was soaked in brandy."

Janet said the woman never paid her the money, despite the fact that she saved her dog. Despite the fact that in saving her dog, Janet suffered second and third-degree burns to over forty percent of her body. Janet said that instead of paying her, the woman sued for damages and emotional distress.

"She had the summons delivered while I was still in the burn unit," Janet said. "They dropped it right on the bed. Can you believe that?"

And I couldn't. I still can't.

I can't do this to Janet.

"You look like you're having doubts," says Dr. Farragut.

"She's my friend," I say.

"And you're concerned about her well-being? Is that it? That's okay. That's a natural concern. But it's a concern that also, I think, comes from a place of limited knowledge. Because, are there some factors you aren't privy to? Are there some elements about Janet's situation you may not be aware of? There are. Did you know that Janet's girlfriend—or whatever it is she and Sheila are calling one another—runs a lucrative podiatry practice? Yes, indeed. There's good money in feet. Everybody has them. So, financially speaking, I'd say she's good. Plus, if Janet wants another job, she'll have no problem finding one. Because you know what, not hiring people like her is almost as bad as firing them?"

Then Dr. Farragut does a kind of sideways lean and checks his hair in the reflection of his computer monitor. "Why are we even talking about Janet?" he says. "Why aren't we talking about you? About your future well-being? About the wealth of quality assignments that will soon be coming your way? I hear the Guadalupe fur seal isn't doing so well. How'd you like a crack at one of those?"

Then Dr. Farragut points behind him, to his framed cover of *Conservation Quarterly.* In the photo, he has a strong, confident smile. Even the ocelot looks happier than I can remember being.

"That could be you in a few months," he says. "Would you like that?"

I would. I know I shouldn't. I know the focus should be on the animals, but after everything that's happened, everything I've been through, don't I deserve a break?

I think I do.

"What do you have in mind?" I say.

"I have a plan."

First, Dr. Farragut announces that we'll have an extra Collection Day on Thursday. So, on Thursday, I push the Collection Cart around the facility. I collect any extra samples from Release, and any leftover samples from Insemination, and bring them to Cryogenics to freeze for later use.

As always, Monroe stops me and examines an Extraction Container. He gives it a swirl. He gives it a sniff. He guesses at the species of the sample, and, as always, he's wrong.

But this time, I tell him he's correct. Monroe is overjoyed. He actually swoons a bit and almost spills the sample. I take the Extraction Container from him and help him find a seat. I tell him to breathe.

Then doubt creeps in. Monroe questions his ability. He says he wants to see the label. Instead, I praise his unique insights and understanding of the animal kingdom. I suggest, to celebrate said insights and understanding, Monroe allow me to take him to lunch. Then, I run a finger across his chest and say, "I always knew there was something special about you."

This last part is Dr. Farragut's suggestion.

Of course Monroe says yes. Of course he never bothers to check the label, which has been blank the entire time.

While we're gone, Dr. Farragut sneaks into the Cryo Lab and steals some samples.

It takes Monroe a few hours to notice they're missing. Then he reports the missing samples, and, per protocol, Dr. Farragut calls for a facility-wide search.

Sample theft has been a major concern since the Rusty Torson scandal. Rusty was stealing Bengal tiger samples and selling them to Chinese businessmen with virility issues. What they did with them is anyone's guess, but it's not something I care to think about.

We make a show of searching the entire facility. Then we get to Janet's office where, of course, we find the samples in her filing cabinet.

Janet tries denying everything, but Dr. Farragut cuts her off. He condemns her selfishness. He chastises her ability to play fast and loose with the future of the animal kingdom. Then he makes a comparison to a pirate on Noah's ark, which is ineffective and, frankly, a bit much.

Finally, two guys from Control come in. They flank Janet and march her from her office. They don't even allow her to pack her things.

As she passes by, she doesn't say a word. She just stares at me the entire time. Right at me. Right through me. And even though her face doesn't move, doesn't display any emotion, I know that she knows.

Then the three of them turn the corner and disappear.

"Well," Dr. Farragut says, "I'm glad that ordeal is over. I, for one, feel better. Lighter somehow."

"Not me. I feel empty. Like I've been hollowed out."

"That's a kind of lighter," he says. "Look, did I say this would be easy? Or pleasant? No. But it's done now, and the important thing, the necessary thing, is to get over it and move on."

Maybe he's right. No, he's definitely right. I need to focus on the here and now. I need to think about my pending promotion and upcoming assignments. I need to find some solace in the fact that I am finally free from toads and frogs.

"So no more standing around on company time with that sad-sack face," Dr. Farragut says. "One of us still has a toad to release."

Then he smacks me on the back and walks away.

Before I head down to Animal Enclosures, I go to my office and do some research on the Puerto Rican crested toad. Their population numbers are in free-fall. It's predicted that without serious conservation efforts, the toads will be extinct in less than a decade.

Though no one can say exactly why. There are no environmental factors threatening their habitat. No rise in predators. Their food supply hasn't dwindled, and, in fact, has increased in some areas. It seems that the toads have simply decided to stop mating.

The scientists are baffled. But maybe they're overlooking something. Something not as simple as mating or not mating.

Maybe the toads have looked at the day-to-day makeup of their lives, the pressures and responsibilities, and realized that they are no longer living, no longer thriving, but merely surviving. Merely enduring for some unknown reason. Maybe they're no longer hopeful about the future. Maybe they've realized that to experience love and happiness, to really let it in, is to leave yourself unguarded. To leave yourself vulnerable to betrayals, and indignities, and the inherent, self-serving nature of others. And so maybe they've said, *Thanks but no thanks. We are no longer interested in this world. We've had enough.*

Probably not though. They're just toads after all.

I head down to Animal Enclosures. I walk past Duncan, and he stares at me as if he'd like to claw my eyes out, and I think: Get in line, big guy.

When I get to the toad, I see he has slightly burrowed himself near the front left corner of his terrarium. His snout is pressed against the glass, and his cream-colored vocal sac vibrates at a steady, rapid rhythm. As I reach in to grab him, his golden irises contract, narrowing his pupils into fine, black lines. He looks like he wants to be left alone.

He looks like Janet did before they took her away.

As I prep him for release, I think about how I got here. A choice was given to me. A choice about who I was willing to use, how much of them I was willing to take. Then I made that choice and justified the decision by saying it was part of a "greater good."

That's what I did

God help me, that's what I do.

Cry on Command

Somber, graceful mourning, with maybe the occasional tear or two, that's one hundred. We call it a Dry. Hysterical crying, with the wailing and the moaning and the classic rhetorical questions screamed to the heavens—the *How could you*'s, the *Why now*'s—that's going to cost you two-fifty. We call those, and really any tear-related mourning, a Wet. Some weeks, Feldman will assign me nothing but Dries. Others, it will be one Wet after another. Those weeks can be exhausting.

Occasionally we'll get a client that requests the "Grecian Widow." They want to see me insane with grief, destroyed by loss, throwing myself on the casket and threatening to jump into the grave. Those can run upwards of five hundred.

Not that I get anything close to that. What I get is ten to fifty dollars a funeral, plus tips. Not that anyone tips. You'd think Feldman would at least reimburse me for expenses. Like the mascara I go through after a week of Wets. Like my dry cleaning. *Black doesn't show stains,* he likes to remind me, and yes, generally it doesn't. But when you're crawling through freshly turned earth in a dress already damp with tears, it tends to leave a mark.

The only expense Feldman covers are the forget-me-nots I lay on each casket before it's lowered in the ground. Forget-me-nots, of course, being the official flower of the professional mourner.

Monday, I get to the office five minutes late, but just in time to get nearly tackled by some woman reeling through the lobby. She's young, maybe half my age, and pretty, though it's hard to tell with the wide-eyed look of panic on her face.

"What's with her?" I ask Evelyn, our Receptionist and Bookings Coordinator.

"Failed the Fish Test."

I look again at the woman. She's wearing black heels and a matching sleeveless dress. The dress still has the tags on it.

Of course. The Fish Test. Potential mourners-for-hire don't come in to interview so much as audition. After making them stew in the lobby for a few minutes, Feldman invites them into his office. On his desk is a small fish tank. It's a nice tank. It has colored rocks and a plant. It has one of those little treasure chests that periodically burps out bubbles. And, swimming inside, it has a solitary clown fish.

"This is Nemo," Feldman tells them.

"Like from that movie?" they say.

"Like from that movie," Feldman says.

The fish's name is an obvious and intentional reference. People get it, and it makes them feel intelligent. Confident. They smile. They relax a little. In some small way, a bond is formed. This is key.

"Can you cry on command?" Feldman says.

This question comes right from our ad. At the bottom, in bold letters it reads: THOSE THAT CANNOT CRY ON COMMAND NEED NOT APPLY.

They say yes. Every applicant says yes.

Feldman says, "Let's see." Then he reaches into the tank and grabs the fish. "Follow me," he tells them.

They walk into the bathroom.

"Welcome to Nemo's funeral," Feldman says. "You're distraught. Overcome with grief. Let me see it. Lay it on me." Then he drops

Nemo into the toilet. Both watch as Nemo swims a few disoriented laps around the bowl. Then Feldman flushes.

Almost everyone fails. I suppose it's the spontaneity or shock of it all. It's too much. People freeze up. Most people.

"If you can't cry for this fish," Feldman says, "this fish who, less than a minute ago, embodied the inane reference you so valued, then how can you possibly cry for a complete stranger?"

It's a fair question. It's at that point most people grab their things and go.

What they don't know, not that it would help them with their grief problem, is that the toilet's a prop. It's not connected to the sewer. Nemo, the water, all come out of a pipe on the other side of the wall and empty into a bucket. On average, Nemo "dies" four to five times a week.

When I first started working here, some of the other employees were quick to praise Feldman's humanity, his respect for God's creatures. But Feldman doesn't not kill the fish because he's a humane animal lover. Feldman doesn't not kill the fish because he's a cheap bastard.

The woman in black is still outside of our lobby. She's hunched over by the bushes and crying now. Sobbing really. It's a messy, mucus-heavy type of crying. Every few seconds, she wipes her face, and then wipes her hands on her dress.

She better be careful, or the store won't take it back.

"Sure," Feldman says, walking over, Nemo's bucket sloshing in his hand. "Now she can cry. What a waste. Nothing worse than seeing a woman cry for free."

When Feldman first started this business, it was simply about addressing attendance concerns. Maybe the deceased was new to the area and hadn't made a lot of friends. Maybe their relatives were far away or, in some cases, no longer living. Either way, a low turnout was expected, and nobody wants a poorly attended funeral.

But soon word got around. Soon, it became about more than just attendance. People realized they could transfer their grief. They could hire someone to provide the requisite amount of sadness and suffering while maintaining their composure. Their refinement. Because when someone dies, the human custom and social obligation to mourn their loss still exists, but for those at a certain tax bracket, there's a level of grieving that is, apparently, unbecoming.

That's where we come in.

Feldman likes to remind us that we're more than professional mourners; we're grief surrogates. Through us, people are able to display their loss. Through us, they're able to pay their respects.

But sometimes I'm not so sure. Sometimes I think I'm perpetuating this myth that people can be insulated from loss, from sadness. Sometimes I think I'm just another way for them to avoid reality.

According to my schedule, I have two Dries and four Wets this week, beginning with a Level III Wet this afternoon. Technically, a Level III is "high-pitched, stuttering sobs with continuous tears," but around the office, we call it Chipmunk Crying.

It costs one seventy-five.

The deceased is a Mr. Miles Hoglund, the former President and CEO of something called Hog-Smart Industries. It makes me think of a bunch of pigs in lab coats staring intently into microscopes, though that's probably not accurate.

His graveside service is well-attended, which suggests that he was popular with his employees, or that attendance was mandatory.

I'm situated off to the side, next to the casket and a large photo of Mr. Hoglund on an easel. In it, he has thick, silver hair and bushy eyebrows. A playful smile. He looks like he was a kind man.

After everyone has settled in, a priest reads a few passages from the Bible. Then he tells us not to mourn for Mr. Hoglund, that he is spending eternity living in the house of the Lord. He tells us our job is to continue to find glory and salvation here, the land of the living.

As he talks, I watch a bird peck at a malt liquor bottle someone has dumped in the weeds growing around a crooked tombstone.

The priest finishes, and then a man stands and addresses the crowd. He's tall and lean and emits a health club glow. His cologne is penetrating.

"Today, we say goodbye to a great man. A pillar of the community and the bedrock of our work family. To me, and I'm sure you'll all agree, Mr. Hoglund wasn't just a boss. He was a mentor. A father-figure really. Because doesn't a father protect and provide for his family? That was Mr. H to a tee. Remember when we had that spat of break-ins and muggings in the common lot of employee parking? Who was it that made sure each and every one of you got a pepper-spray keychain in your stocking at the Christmas party? Even Stephanie Goldfarb got one, didn't you? Where are you, Steph?"

Everyone turns in their plastic folding chairs as a woman in a black cardigan slowly raises her hand while lowering her head.

"You weren't overlooked or forgotten just because you don't believe in Christmas. And why was that? Because Mr. Hoglund didn't discriminate. And he listened. Like a good father, Mr. Hoglund listened to his family. When we had a few rough quarters and the austerity measures began to take hold, who heard your concerns? Who, in less than three month's time, reinstituted complimentary toilet paper in almost every restroom? You know, every day I took comfort in the knowledge that Mr. Hoglund was up on thirty-three, protecting us and listening to us. Watching over us. And he still is. He's still up there.

Sure, he's up a little higher now, probably playing golf with Reagan, but he's still there. Mr. Hoglund is still there for you. Now, like then, his door is always open. Except now of course you don't have to make an appointment and have Margery escort you on to the executive elevator. So now, as we undergo a transition and I attempt to fill some very large shoes, I want all of you to still feel free to talk to Mr. Hoglund. Discuss your concerns. Share your problems. Try to keep these talks brief, or even better, save them until you've clocked out, but still, don't feel that you have to come to *me* with every little issue. Maybe, instead, allow Mr. H to continue to be the father of our work family. Our father, in heaven. Now let's all give him a big hand."

Then everyone applauds. Everyone but me. I just cry.

When people hear about my job, the first things they ask are, *How do you do it? How do you cry on command? And so easily? Do you think of sad things?* And sure, some of us do. Some mourners maintain a mental catalogue of sad images. A three-legged puppy. An orphan with a lisp. An orphan, who upon being asked if they'd like a puppy, regardless of the missing leg issue, responds with an overjoyed, *Yes, pwease!*

Everyone has their triggers. The important thing is to find what works for you.

Other mourners rely on performance enhancement techniques. They'll rub dish soap in their eyes. Hide bits of raw onion in their handkerchiefs. Some pinch themselves through their dress. Others pluck a nose hair or two.

Me, I just think about the fact that I'm a fifty-year-old widow, that my late husband had been lying to me for the majority of our marriage, and now, because of that, our business and savings are gone, and my job is to cry at strangers' funerals.

I think of that, and I have no problem crying.

The day my husband died, he was attending a groundbreaking ceremony for our second restaurant. Just after he and some of the other investors put on the matching hardhats, stuck their shovels into the ground, and smiled for the camera, Gene collapsed. He had a heart attack. They said he was dead within minutes.

A few weeks later a young man called asking if I'd like a copy of the photo. The photo of my husband right before he died? Who would want such a thing? I was furious. I called that young man some names I now regret.

Then I called back and asked him to please send me the picture.

I still haven't been able to look at it.

Gene and I met almost twenty years ago. On our first date, he told me his dream was to start a business combining the two great loves of his life. I used to think that at some point I made it to the top of that list, but those first two: Catholicism and Chinese food.

Gene told me he experienced it for the first time while vacationing in San Francisco. He was in some hot and crowded dive in a back alley of the Tenderloin, and after that first mouthful, he was hooked.

Chinese food that is. Not Catholicism.

I've tried here and there to get into it, but I never really developed a taste for it. I think part of the problem's that it was forced upon me as child.

Catholicism, that is. Not Chinese food.

But Gene was so passionate, so determined. His enthusiasm was infectious, and truth be told, I was falling in love.

So I agreed to help.

Gene and I worked hard, and we saved, and nine years later we opened our first Wok With Jesus.

Our first, and now it seems, our last. Things have been difficult since Gene passed. I've missed two mortgage payments, and now the bank is talking foreclosure and has started repossessing assets. I tried increasing revenue. I tried coupons and circulars. I tried a deal where kids eat free on Wednesdays. We had some dedicated customers from the church, but then Burton Hoover, our day manager, was arrested. By the FBI. It seems that between greeting customers and politely inquiring if they were "right with the Lord"—a practice I never endorsed—and wishing them a "blessed day" on their way out, he was slowly filling the office computer's hard drive with child pornography. The FBI confiscated the computer and ordered the store closed pending an investigation.

So the church people are gone, and the investors have pulled out, and any hopes of revenue are a moot point.

I'm halfway home from the Hoglund funeral when I realize tonight's my turn to make dinner. I stop off at the restaurant to heat up a few things. Might as well use what's left before it goes bad. Before the bank takes the rest of it.

We're down to our last wok, and the gas company has cut us off, so I'm forced to use some Sterno cans to cook the food. Needless to say, it's slow going. I wander around the restaurant to pass the time.

I imagine when the bank takes over and this place eventually becomes another Walgreens or Starbucks, the first thing they'll do is paint over the mural.

Before our grand opening, Gene commissioned a local artist to paint a mural of Jesus between the two buffet stations. The artist rendered Him in the style of The Last Supper—arms out, palms up—as if to indicate the varied and bountiful array of Chinese delicacies. Or so I assume. Gene loved it, but I've always thought something wasn't quite right. The lips are too pursed, and the eyes are too narrow, and the whole thing gives off an impression of judgment. As if He knows our General Tso's chicken is more breading than meat. Or that our egg drop soup comes from a mix. And sure, that's all true, but to me, it's easy to pass judgment when one doesn't have to deal with rising food costs. Not all of us can take a few fish and some bread and feed the masses.

Gene wanted to have the artist come back later and add some scripture. Something relevant. Something about ye eating and drinking in the glory of the Lord. But he never did. I talked him out of it. I thought it was an unnecessary expense, and, ultimately, we put the money towards a soft-serve ice cream machine.

The bank took the ice cream machine last Friday.

When the food is cooked, I box it up and take one last look around. The desk in the office looks so much bigger without the computer. Hanging on the wall is the first dollar we made. Gene had it framed. On the bottom is a plaque with the date and this inscription: *The realization of a dream. The support of a best friend.*

I take the frame from the wall, break the glass on a corner of the desk, and shove the dollar into my purse.

Goddamn you, Gene.

When I get home, it takes me another ten minutes to find parking because I have to park in the street. Because there's a Windstar in my driveway. The Windstar belongs to my sister Constance and her husband. It's their RV. I'm sure in its day the Windstar was the height of recreational travel technology, but it's long past its prime. Like a lot of us. Its once gold paint has suffered decades of sun bleaching, and now it more closely resembles the color of unbrushed teeth.

Connie and Warren were in the middle of crisscrossing America when Gene died, so they postponed their trip to attend the service and help out. They've been here ever since. I know they're ready to get back on the road, and part of me is ready for them to go, but I also know Connie is worried about leaving me alone.

Truth be told, I'm a little worried about being left alone.

Neither of us knows what to do, and we're not really talking about it, so until then, the Windstar's hulking, leaking mass will continue to sit in my driveway, its back end blocking the sidewalk, its right-side tires ruining my lawn.

Connie meets me at the front door. She's wearing another one of her T-shirts. At some point, Connie's entire wardrobe has been replaced by souvenir T-shirts from the various stops of their trip. Yesterday's shirt featured a cowboy hat warning me not to "Mess with Texas." Tonight, it's one from their Mount Rushmore trip, with a picture of the monument emblazoned across her chest.

Connie's husband is already seated at the dining room table.

"How are you, Warren?"

"Hungry."

"Well, dinner's right here," I say, holding up the take-out boxes.

"Chinese food. What a surprise."

We spend the first few minutes eating in relative silence, the room filling with the clinking of silverware and the way Warren chews his food so that everything sounds crunchy regardless of its consistency.

"Have either of you talked to Mindy lately?" I say.

Warren grunts out a lungful of air and throws his fork to his plate, where it plops in a pile of shrimp lo mein with little dramatic effect.

"Did I say something wrong?"

"No," Connie says. "It's just Mindy's new job. It's got Warren a touch perturbed."

"My daughter's selling her body like a common whore," he says.

"Warren, she is not," Connie says.

"She lays with strange men."

"She snuggles them," Connie reminds him. And then to me says,

"She's cuddling people. It's a healing practice. Oriental, I think. They say it's very therapeutic. Plus, it's certified."

"It's for the best you and Gene couldn't have kids," Warren says.

Actually, it wasn't so much we couldn't, as we just didn't. There was always the restaurant to think of, and concerns about money. Time got away from us, and we just never did. Then at some point, we changed *didn't* to *couldn't*. We both knew it wasn't true, but somehow it made us feel better. I've never told Connie that, and I'm sure as hell not telling Warren now.

"Because kids will break your heart," he continues. "Sure, they start off as your little angel, as Daddy's little girl, but before you know it they're all grown up, and then they spread their legs and fly away."

"Oh my," Connie says, putting a hand to her chest, covering Roosevelt and half of Jefferson. "Darling, I think you mean wings."

"What?"

"Wings. They spread their wings and fly away."

"No. I don't."

Then Warren stands, grabs his plate, and informs us that he'll be in the Windstar. When he's gone, I ask Connie if she remembers Tammy Newton from high school.

"No, I don't believe so."

"Sure you do," I say. "Tammy Newton. She was in Ms. Marr's Algebra class with us. Red head. Sort of a heavy-set girl."

Connie shrugs with her face.

"She was always eating *those* cookies and telling everyone how her great-grandfather founded the company. All of the kids called her Pig Newton."

"Sorry," Connie says. "It doesn't ring a bell. What about her?"

"She's dead. I'm working her funeral on Saturday."

After dinner, I head upstairs and lie down. I watch some TV. The Monday Night Movie is some awful remake of *Citizen Kane* where the title character is even more bloated than in the original, and, for some reason, Scottish.

I change the channel. I change the channel, and there he is—standing before a pulpit with his two-tone pompadour and ridiculous goatee, his fat face contorted into a mask of sanctimony—Roland Ravanel.

Ravanel is one of the more successful televangelists preaching something called the Prosperity Gospel, which centers on the concept of Seed Faith. Practitioners of Seed Faith believe they can sow seeds, which symbolize their belief and devotion to God, which, in turn, increases the power of His love and the likelihood He'll answers their prayers.

Even now, Ravanel is pounding a fist to the pulpit, imploring his followers to increase the amount of their seeds, so when their inevitable harvest comes in, it will be all the more miraculous. Then the camera pans over to a giant stained-glass eagle, its wings spread, a golden cross in its talons.

Of course, "seeds" mean money, and "sowing them" means sending that money to Ravanel's church, and the only miracle is that Gene had been doing this for the last twelve years and I had no idea.

I found out after he died. Gene handled all of the finances—the mortgages, the bills, the books for the restaurant—all of them. Then when I took over, I learned he'd given away almost everything we had.

In the days following Gene's funeral, I remember being paralyzed at the thought of having to go through his things, the memories and pain they'd trigger, and how, in an instant, I went from that to ripping his jackets and suits from their hangers and dumping out his dresser drawers.

That's how I found the letters. In shoe boxes beneath Gene's side of the bed were hundreds of letters. All of them from Pastor Roland

Ravanel and his Garden of Faith Ministry. All of them congratulating Gene on his devotion, confirming his ever-growing place in God's heart, and compelling him to send more. All of them addressed to a post office box I had never heard of.

I called the Ministry demanding to speak to someone in charge, demanding some answers. I was transferred four times and made to listen to over an hour's worth of upbeat Christian Muzak. Then Ravanel himself came on the line. He told me that Gene's contributions were of his own volition. That it was all perfectly legal. Then he said the amount of seed Gene had sown over the years had been considerable, and he was undoubtedly enjoying a glorious place in heaven beside the Lord. He said this, I suppose, thinking it would make me feel better.

It did not.

Then Ravanel wished me a "blessed day" and hung up. That's how Connie found me—the bedroom torn upside-down, Gene's things scattered everywhere, and me sitting in the middle of the floor, crying and screaming at the phone. She sat down with me, wrapped her arms around my shoulders, dried my face on her T-shirt.

It told me that "Everything's Peachy in Georgia."

Now Ravanel, microphone in hand, is pacing the cobalt blue carpet of his stage. He's asking his followers if they're lost, and in pain, and desperate for relief. "Wouldn't you like to know that these sorrows and struggles aren't yours alone to carry?" he says.

The show cuts to members of the audience crying and nodding their heads.

Then Ravanel starts crying, too. His expression morphs into a doughy swell of pity and manufactured tears leak from his beady black eyes.

But it's not real. He's just aping their grief. He's just capitalizing on their needs and the hollow promise he can take their pain away.

I spend the rest of the night lying awake, trying to convince myself that Ravanel and I are not one in the same. That our roles, our intentions, are different. But I can't. The similarities are too numerous, too painfully obvious. Accepting it is only a matter of time.

It doesn't mean it makes me feel better.

First thing Tuesday morning is a pet funeral. Our rates for an animal service are the same as a human's. Our price point depends on the degree of mourning, the amount of physicality in our grief, not what's in the box. Most animal service clients request a standard Dry, or maybe a Level I Wet—silent, yet streaming tears—but what they really want is some company. As they say their final goodbye to what is likely the last companion they had in the world, they simply don't want to be alone.

Some of the other mourners complain when Feldman assigns them a pet funeral. They think it's beneath them. But not me. I don't mind. The way I see it, these animals were loved, and were as much a part of these people's lives as any other family member. In some cases, even more so. Plus, I've always found it easier to cry for animals than people.

When I get back to the office, I see Evelyn crying at her desk. At first, I think she is considering some work in the field, and maybe practicing her technique. But no. Her grief is real. As she collects her things and puts them in a box, Evelyn tells me she made a mistake with the anniversary mailers.

For an extra twelve dollars, we'll send a remembrance card on the anniversary of a loved one's passing. Evelyn says that in our latest mail out, there was a bit of a mix-up. It seems she accidently sent the card intended for the family of Bentley Morris, a golden retriever, to the former home of Bradley Morris, the deceased son of Craig and Susan

Morris. I say that doesn't sound so bad. Then Evelyn tells me that Bradley was severely epileptic and died of a grand mal seizure. Then she hands me a copy of the card. It reads: *On this day, know that your little Bradley is in Heaven, thinking about you, and wagging his tail.*

Evelyn says Feldman has discontinued the service, and to absorb the revenue loss, he's letting her go. I know she's struggling. Not only is she raising two little girls on her own, but the younger one has some sort of foot issue—no arch, or too much of an arch, I forget which—and has to limp around in a corrective boot.

I march down to Feldman's office, but he doesn't want to hear it. He says Susan Morris is some bigwig on the Chamber of Commerce, and the word of mouth alone could ruin us. He says an example needs to be made. He says it's out of his hands.

Still, I continue to protest, but Feldman waves a Client File in my face.

"I know you're upset," he says. "Good. Go use it."

Then he hands me the file and tells me not to be late.

It's another rich guy's funeral. Late sixties. Millions in the bank. Died on his catamaran. His four kids from his three marriages are here, but none of them looks too bereaved about Dad's death. Honestly, they seem a bit bored. The current wife is here as well, though she looks young enough to be one of the kids.

A trophy-wife client always makes for a difficult job. They still want someone else to do the messy work of grieving, but they don't want to be overshadowed or out-mourned.

Like this one. Even though the wife requested and paid for a Level III Wet, throughout the service, she keeps giving me this look. She keeps narrowing her eyes and furrowing her otherwise unlined face as if to say, *Hey, reign it in a little.*

So I reign it in a little. I give her what she wants. I know my place. I may appear to mourn for the dead, but I cry for the living.

The thing about being a professional mourner is that the job is almost entirely physical, and, over time, that physicality becomes habitual. Muscle memory takes over. It allows the mind to wander.

I think about the people who send Ravanel money, the people who attend his services. Almost all of them are extremely ill, or the loved ones of an ill person. They're hoping to be saved from Parkinson's, or have their paralysis cured, or be free from cancer. They're hoping for a miracle. But not Gene. Gene wasn't sick. Even his heart attack came as a surprise to his doctor. So what was it? What was it about our life that he was so desperate and determined to fix? That he felt he needed a miracle to do so? And how did I not see any of it? What was he looking for, and why couldn't he just talk to me?

When I get back to the office, the lights are off and everyone's gone. Evelyn's desk has been cleared of her photos and postcards and little knickknacks, and I realize I never said goodbye.

There's a note on Feldman's door saying he's closed early to do some damage control about the Morris debacle. He reminds me that we have a DistaGrieve service in the morning, and that he'll be operating one of the cameras to insure it goes smoothly and one more thing doesn't get "cocked up." How lovely. What lovely language. When I remove the note, the door opens a crack, and I see the light from Nemo's tank is on. So I go in and sit at Feldman's desk and watch him swim for a while.

I never had to take the Fish Test.

Before all of this, before Gene died, and before Ravanel and the money problems, Feldman was one of our customers. He'd usually come in alone, sit in the back corner of the restaurant, and read the paper—the obituaries, of course—while he ate. Afterwards, I'd bring him his check, and then he'd ask for a to-go box, and then I would explain the nature of a buffet.

Then, one night, Feldman came by just after I'd locked up. I was still reeling from the Ravanel news. Burton had been arrested that afternoon. The restaurant was technically shut down, and I wasn't supposed to have any customers, but I was too tired to care. I let him in. Feldman helped himself to what was left of the buffet, but instead of going to his usual table, he sat with me. He asked what was wrong.

"What makes you think something is wrong?" I said.

"Have you seen your face?" he said.

So while Feldman ate, I told him everything.

At first, he didn't say anything. He just sat there, playing with the remnants of his beef and broccoli. "Huh," he finally said. "What is it that they say? 'What doesn't kill us makes us stronger?'"

"I think that's bullshit. It's a lie we tell ourselves to feel better."

"Yeah," he said. "Probably. But still, bad things happen, and though they may not make you stronger, if you're smart, they can make you money."

Then Feldman asked if I cried at Gene's funeral.

"Of course," I said.

"And now? Knowing everything that you do, everything that he did, could you cry for him now?"

I thought about it. I admitted that though I had cried for Gene since I learned what he'd done, it had been different. It wasn't grief exactly, but something else.

Then Feldman smiled and asked if I was looking for work.

Our DistaGrieve service is Feldman's latest innovation. For an extra ninety-five dollars, we'll record the ceremony and then burn the footage to a DVD for family members who want to attend the service, but don't have the time or the money.

Today, that seems to mean everyone. The entire family. Feldman and I are the only ones here. There's the deceased, of course. And Father Bryan from St. Luke's, but he doesn't count. He's essentially a professional just like us.

Feldman hands me a video camera. "Keep your shots tight," he says. "Zoom in a lot. Let's not advertise the fact that there's not too many people here."

"There's no one here," I say, but Feldman waves this off. He tells me to get some footage of the tombstone.

So I get some footage of the tombstone.

It reads: *Gone but not forgotten.*

I get some more shots of questionable usefulness: the leaden sky, the treetops swaying in the breeze, two squirrels fighting over an empty Doritos bag.

Then Feldman says it's time to begin the service. He positions one camera on a tripod in front of Father Bryan and the casket. The other, he handholds a few feet from me.

"Okay," he whispers, "go ahead. Mourn."

I go through my routine. I think about how it felt to lose something only to learn none of it was real. I think about the times I catch Connie staring at me, and the way she smiles, and how I know it's love but feels more like pity. I think about the future.

But it doesn't work. Nothing happens. I scrunch my eyes tight, try to squeeze the tears out, but nothing comes.

"What's the problem?" Feldman says.

I shake my head.

"What is that? What does that mean?"

"I don't know," I say. "I can't do it. I can't cry."

"Jesus Christ," Feldman yells.

Father Bryan clears his throat, checks his watch.

"I don't need this right now," Feldman says. "Just try harder. You can do it. You're better than this."

But I'm not sure I am.

"Why didn't I ever have to take the Fish Test?" I say.

"What?"

"I'm the only one, right? So why me? Why didn't I have to take it?"

"I don't know. You didn't need it."

"What? What does that mean?"

Feldman sighs and stares at the ground, scanning it from left to right as if the answer is etched into the dirt and he is unable to find it. The camera, though still pointed at me, begins to droop in his hands. "Do you remember the night I offered you a job?" he says. "I asked if you had cried for your husband after everything that had happened?"

"Yes. So?"

"And you told me that you had. In spite of what he did, in spite of what you thought you knew about him, about your marriage, you still cried. Don't you get it? You've been crying for strangers since the beginning."

He's right. He's right, and the truth of it hits me like something physical, something real. Like something I haven't felt in a long time. And even though it's the saddest, most pathetic-sounding thing I've ever heard, and even though the cameras are rolling, and Feldman and Father Bryan are staring at me, I can't help but laugh.

And laugh.

And laugh.

Understudy to a Matinee Jesus

In the beginning, God created the heavens and the earth. Or so they say. My beginning, at least as BibleLand goes, was not so impressive. Michael called the night before my first day. He said it would take a while to process my employee-parking pass, and until then, I should park with the tour buses and shuttle vans, right beside the Sea of Galilee Miracle and Photo Opportunity.

"The what?" I said. "What does that mean?"

"What do you mean 'what does that mean?' You got some kind of problem with that particular biblical experience?"

"What? No. I—"

"Sorry," he said. "I'm sorry. If I seem a bit defensive it's because the Sea of Galilee Miracle was mine. My idea. Ravanel loved it, and he green-lit it immediately, only to betray me in the end. That Judas. Even so, we must accept and overcome these challenges, and continue to try to live in Christ's image."

"Sure," I said.

"The park opens at ten," Michael said. "So get here a few minutes before, and I'll show you around. I'll wait for you in parking."

And this morning, when I pull onto the lot, there he is. I've never met Michael before, but even if he weren't the only person standing in an empty parking lot, he'd be easy enough to spot. He's the one who looks like Jesus. He's got the long hair and the beard. He's got the white robe with the blue sash. He also appears to be standing beside a statue of himself.

"So," Michael says, "what do you think?"

Florida's Interstate 4 looms large over the park, and on the wall of one of the exit ramps is a mural of a sunset rendered in the requisite purples and pinks and golds. On the ground is a reflective sheet of navy blue Lucite with tiny whitecaps intermittently detailed in. And, standing in the center, is a plaster statue of Jesus. The effect is that if you stand just so, and leave your logic in the car, it does look like Jesus walking on water.

"It's cool," I say. "Very impressive."

"Thank you," Michael says. "The idea came to me in a moment of divine inspiration, so I can't take all of the credit. But, of course, you see the problem, right?" Then, from somewhere in the folds of his robe, he produces a pack of cigarettes. Michael smokes the kind of long, thin cigarettes you normally see dangling from the lips of Bingo Night grandmas. He lights up. "Take a good look," he says.

This feels like a test. I've never been good at tests, and this one, loaded as it is with first-day jitters, is an unwelcomed development.

As the roar of cars and trucks headed to Tampa sound overhead, I stare at the Sea of Galilee Miracle and Photo Opportunity. I stare at the sunset mural. I stare at the statue of Jesus, arms out, ready to pose with guests. And all the while Michael stares at me, his frustration with my mystery-solving inabilities growing on his face between puffs.

It's weird to watch Jesus smoke.

"I'm sorry," I finally say. "I don't know what you're talking about."

Michael leans in so his face and the statue's are inches apart. "Can't you see it? This statue doesn't look anything like me."

He's right. The statue is a much younger and frankly prettier version of Jesus than Michael's flesh and blood rendition.

"There's a certain likeness," I say, but Michael waves this off. Then he takes a final drag of his cigarette and rubs it out on the statue's cheek. Then we walk to the main gate and officially enter BibleLand Adventures and Museum.

BibleLand Adventures is a subsidiary of Pastor Roland Ravanel and his Garden of Faith Ministry. Ravanel is a nationally syndicated televangelist. If you've been awake early on Sunday mornings, you've likely seen him in one of his neon suits, pacing back and forth across your television screen, pleading with the Almighty to save your wayward soul.

As Michael and I walk past ticketing, various signs tell me that "BibleLand Adventures and Museum is the most prestigious religious theme park in the greater Orlando area."

The first attraction after ticketing is The Jerusalem Street Market. Here, various employees in period costume stand behind stalls selling wheat and spices and bright pieces of cloth. Other employees pretend to haggle with them over prices. There's lots of furrowed brows and wagging fingers. In the shade of a palm tree, a man struggles to load a basket of figs onto an animatronic donkey.

"Wow," I say. "The customers must love this."

Michael stops walking, turns and stares at me. "Customers? You should know better than that. It was covered in your orientation packet."

Right. This is, I believe, number three of Ravanel's Ten Commandments. Essentially, they're a list of directives for park employees, highlighting areas of concern that, I suppose, the original ten failed to address. Number three commands that we never refer to guests of the park as "customers," but only as "visitors" or something else. I sort of skimmed the packet.

"Travelers," Michael says. "That's my preference. Remember, when people enter our gates they are transported thousands of miles across the globe, and thousands of years into the past, to arrive in first-century Judea."

Then he says something else, but two fire trucks race each other down I-4, and their sirens drown him out.

We move on to the Garden of Gethsemane. It's a shady little nook where visitors can pray, or at least escape the heat of the sun. It has rocks and flowers and music sounding from concealed speakers. Sure, the rocks are plaster, and the flowers are plastic, but it seems peaceful enough. The music sounds like harp.

"Over there," Michael says, pointing to a small, squat building that's been made to look like a temple, "is the Lost and Found."

"Oh yeah," I say. "What's that? Some sanctuary for redemption and salvation?"

"No. It's a Lost and Found. Guy forgets his sunglasses, misplaces his car keys. A Lost and Found. What's the matter with you? Are you some kind of idiot? Because the last guy they gave me was an idiot. One of God's children, yes, of course, but stupid. It was like trying to train a stray dog, except not as cute. So I hope you're not an idiot."

"I'm not."

"Because you're not that cute either."

Then the deep gong of church bells rings out from the P.A. system.

"Let's go," Michael says. "It's showtime."

By the time we return to The Jerusalem Market, a number of visitors have arrived. There's a group of kids in matching T-shirts from some Christian middle school, all of them bored already and lost to their phones. The remaining guests are an even mixture of the elderly and the infirm. Lots of motorized scooters. Wheelchairs. Walkers.

I suddenly notice there's not a single stair in the entire park.

Soon the crowds roll toward an outdoor stage. Michael seats me just off to the side, drops a script in my lap.

"Try to learn something," he says.

The title page tells me this morning's performance is called "The Good Shepherd." This is why I was hired, for my theatrical experience. Before this, I worked for Destination Discovery, the children's science museum. I was in a stage production about health and nutrition. I played Insoluble Fiber, wearing this brown, tube-shaped costume. For the big musical finale, I'd don a hardhat and sing about constructing a healthy digestive system. One day, Ravanel was there with one of his youth groups. He found me after the show and complimented my ability to project so much joy and energy despite having such a pathetic and degrading role. Then he asked if I wanted a job.

"I have a job," I said.

"You're a dancing piece of shit," he said.

Technically, I was fiber, but it didn't matter. He was right. He was right, but somehow it hurt more coming from a man of God.

Ravanel gave me his card. He said I should use my gifts in service to something greater than myself. He said I should call him when I was ready for the big time.

The curtain rises, and "The Good Shepherd" begins. A dozen actors populate a street scene, all of them wearing historically accurate shawls and robes and headdresses. I'm not sure if this is the "big time," but their production value is much better. The science museum never even washed my fiber costume. When I complained about the smell, they said it added to the authenticity. Michael enters from stage left, and the crowd grows excited. He is the rabbi they've heard about. He performs a few miracles—makes a blind man see, a lame guy walk. Then a man from the crowd points to Michael. He says no man should have these powers. He calls him a "demon." Doubt and unrest swell among the would-be followers, but Michael quells this with a rousing speech. He tells them that he is the gate, and that they, the sheep who pass through him, will be saved and find pasture. The sheep/shepherd thing is a metaphor, but there's also some plastic sheep scattered around for effect. Then everyone joins hands for a big song-and-dance number about the proximity of God's kingdom and spreading the good news. Then the curtain drops, and a voice on the P.A. system encourages the audience to peruse the many wonders of the gift shop.

After the show, a few visitors stay behind to take their picture with Michael, ask him for an autograph. When they're gone, I ask Michael what he signs.

"Jesus Christ," he says. "Obviously."

"Obviously."

We go backstage so I can meet some members of the cast. Michael introduces me to Chelsea, a short brunette who plays one of the townspeople and occasionally "Rebekah" when they run the Jacob and Esau production. As we shake hands, I notice that Chelsea wears an unusual amount of rouge on her face, applying it so that it creates a perfect circle on each cheek. She looks like one of Santa's elves. When she leaves to change, Michael says it's been a constant battle between her and Kenny, the stage manager. He keeps reminding her that there wasn't rouge in first-century Judea, and she keeps reminding him that she has poor circulation and needs to add some color to her face.

Michael points to another woman. "That's Melanie," he says. "Steer clear of her. She's a nutjob." Michael says she keeps insisting that the other actresses are going through her things and stealing her tampons. He says that Melanie would like some larger roles, but her accusations aren't winning her any friends.

"She'll never be cast in 'The Crucifixion' if she can't relax about a little blood," he says. "Speaking of, have you seen this monstrosity?"

Michael hands me a program advertising the afternoon crucifixion/resurrection production. It's called "The Ultimate Sacrifice." On the cover is a picture of a young, good-looking Jesus.

"That's Colin," Michael says. He tells me that Colin is rumored to be BibleLand's most expensive acquisition. He says that before this, Colin was over at Disney World, playing the Johnny Depp role in their "Pirates of the Caribbean Live Action Spectacular." Apparently Ravanel had been trying to woo Colin away for months. Then one day, he went over to the Magic Kingdom with a giant bag of money and dropped it at Colin's feet.

"Stole him right out from under the Mouse," Michael says.

I look again at the program. There's something so familiar about Colin. Then it hits me. "This is the guy from your Galilee statue," I say. "It looks just like him."

"Oh, not *like* him," Michael says. "It is him. Ravanel made a mold of his face. Do you know I was here three years before I got my first cardboard cutout? Cardboard! Ravanel was too cheap to have it weather-sealed, so, of course, after the first rainstorm, it was just this ruined pile of pulp. I took it home, worked on it for hours with my hair dryer, but it was never the same."

I nod and try to appear sympathetic.

This feels like a lot to take in for a first day.

"And it's not just the statue," Michael says. "Come with me."

Michael drags me through the park, shows me various cardboard cutouts of Colin as Jesus. There's Colin as Jesus welcoming visitors to the Noah's Ark Two-by-Two Petting Zoo. There's Colin as Jesus in front of the Stations of the Cross Cardio Walk. There's even Colin as Jesus inexplicably riding a motorcycle outside of the women's restroom.

These cutouts, I notice, have all been laminated.

Then Michael takes me to King Solomon's Treasures, one of the park's three gift shops. We walk past the BibleLand T-shirts and coffee mugs and shot glasses, to the toy section where there's an array of plush Jesus dolls. Plush Jesus holding a lamb. Plush Jesus with a halo and angel wings. Even a bloody and beaten plush Jesus on the cross. These, too, all look like Colin.

"Ravanel scrapped all of the old inventory," Michael says. "Had these specially made."

"They really do capture his likeness."

"Yeah," Michael says, staring at one of the dolls. "Ravanel's probably got some giant portrait of Colin hanging in the sweatshop where these are sewn."

"You think?"

"Yes. Yes, I do."

Then Michael tells me to join him on his knees, so we can pray for those poor workers and their wretched lives.

So I kneel down and pray. Or, at least, I stare at Michael while he prays.

We're down there for a few minutes, and then Michael turns to me and says, "You hungry?"

We decide to eat in-park. We go over to The Last Supper Café. I'm expecting historically authentic food, but it's just burgers and corndogs and pizza. When it's my turn to order, I'm still trying to decide.

"I guess I'll get the cheeseburger combo," I say to the girl behind the register. Her nametag reads Becca.

"Do you want the David or Goliath?" she says.

"What's the difference?"

Becca sighs, and then mechanically tells me that the Goliath comes with an extra patty, large fries, and a My Cup Runneth Over free refill. Her eyes never leave the register.

I get the sense that Becca has endured this exchange, this question asked and answered, thousands of times. I can feel the soul-crushing tedium, the monotony of it all. And for some reason, I don't want her to associate me with that. Maybe it's because, though they look tired, Becca's eyes are wonderfully large. Maybe it's because there's an edged beauty to her, a look that suggests if one dares to touch, he will likely get cut. Maybe it's because this is the longest conversation I've had with an attractive woman since God-knows-when. Either way, I want to separate myself from the clawing, needy tourists and their wearisome routine.

"This is my first day," I tell her. "I work here, too."

"There's no employee discount," she says.

When we're finished eating, Michael takes me to BibleLand's Garden of Faith Auditorium. On Sundays, Ravanel tapes and broadcasts his sermons here, but the rest of the week, it's where "The Ultimate Sacrifice" is performed.

Colin, of course, has been cast as Jesus, a development Michael complained about for the entirety of lunch. Michael now plays the Roman Centurion who tortures Jesus and oversees His crucifixion. Maybe it's because he gets to pretend to whip Colin and apply a rubber crown of thorns on his head, but it's a role Michael seems to enjoy more than he probably should.

After the show is over, Michael tells me I'll be playing blind Bartimaeus in the morning production and one of the thieves Jesus is crucified with in the afternoon show. Which is an easy role. I don't even have any lines. Basically, I just hang there.

So that's how I spend my first week: blind and healed in the morning, crucified in the afternoon.

The following Monday afternoon, Michael and I are having lunch. He, as usual, is complaining about Colin while I make my way through my Goliath burger and steal glances at Becca.

"It's ageism is what it is," Michael says. "Sure, Ravanel tried to spin it, told me how Colin will bring in a younger crowd, expand our demographic, but what he really meant was that I'm too old to play Jesus."

I look at Michael. The creases around his eyes are deep enough to hold a coin. Wiry, gray hairs spring from his beard.

"When I pressed him," Michael continues, "Ravanel said it was a matter of *authenticity*," and here Michael attempts to do air quotes, but instead uses all of his fingers. It looks like he's clawing the air. "What a crock. If Ravanel was so concerned about authenticity, he'd sure as hell never let Amber play the Virgin Mary."

I don't know why Michael is upset. He still gets to play Jesus in the morning production, and his centurion role has just as many lines as Colin's, but Michael doesn't want to hear it.

"You'll see," he says. "When years of dedication and devotion are brushed aside, when the happiness you've brought to countless people is forgotten, you'll understand." Then he waves a limp hand at my lunch. "Though if you keep eating that garbage, you'll never even get that chance."

"What does that mean?"

"It means if you ever want to play Jesus, you can't spend all week eating burgers and corndogs. Nobody wants a chubby savior."

Michael's right. I have put on a few pounds. I spend most of the crucifixion scene sucking in my gut so it doesn't flop over my loincloth. In fact, my whole "Judea" look is a bit of a mess. When Ravanel hired me, he said I'd have to grow a beard, and I've been trying. I've been trying, but calling what's happening on my face a "beard" would be the most generous and hopeful of terms. It's more like intermittent patches of stubby, forlorn hair.

"That tummy of yours isn't so much of a problem now because the audience isn't paying attention to you," Michael says. "But if you ever want to be front and center, you might think about eating the occasional salad."

I do think about it. "Maybe I won't have to take my clothes off," I say.

"What?"

"You know, like, stay covered up."

"You want to keep your shirt on?" Michael yells. "You want to be the first Jesus to get crucified with His shirt on? You're playing the Messiah, the Son of God, not the fat kid at the public pool!"

Other customers in the café stop eating to stare at us. Even Becca leans over the counter to see what's going on.

I resolve to go on a diet.

With that, Michael tells me about his plan to retake the Jesus role in the afternoon production.

"All we need to do is convince the visitors to see me in more of a Christ-like fashion," he says.

"We?"

"Once they do," he continues, "they'll demand to see me as Jesus again. Ravanel will have to comply."

"Why would I do this?" I say. "I don't want to do this."

Michael sighs and then does this thing with his eyes where they go all liquid and gentle. I've seen him give the same look when he's signing autographs.

"Ravanel, though misguided in his approach, was not entirely wrong," Michael says. "I can't play Jesus forever. One day, I will have to retire. And when I do, I'd like to pass on the role to someone who can fully inhabit it. Someone who appreciates and understands the responsibilities. Not some pretty-boy actor who uses his Jesus part to pick up women."

There's a scene during the resurrection finale where Colin stands on top of a giant plaster boulder, singing about the glory of God, while the rest of us dance beneath him. And maybe it's because he's wearing a robe so white it looks like it emits light, or maybe it's the way the music swells, or the power of the moment, but I've seen the way some of the female cast members look at him afterwards. Maybe Becca would look at me that way.

"So what do you have in mind?" I say. "How do you make the guests see you as more Christ-like?"

"I'm going to start healing them."

"What?"

"I'm going to heal their afflictions in Jesus's name. Doesn't the Bible tell us that if we believe in Jesus and the works He does, we, too, will be able to perform those works? Doesn't it tell us that if we ask for anything in Jesus's name, He will grant it?"

"I have no idea."

"Well, it does. Come on."

Outside of the Garden of Faith Auditorium is a courtyard. Astroturf covers the ground, and Roman statuary lines the perimeter. There are even a couple of employees dressed as Roman centurions, wandering around and posing with guests for pictures. This is where Michael takes me. He surveys the various guests, and then settles on a couple that appear to be in their late seventies. He is dressed entirely in khaki, and the baby blue of her Capri pants is the exact shade of her hair.

"Pardon me," Michael says to the man, "but I was wondering if you suffer from any pain?"

This, given the general age and condition of our clientele, is a loaded question. Of course the man says yes. Then he goes on to describe issues with his feet—bone spurs and trouble with his arches.

"Would you like me to heal them?" Michael says.

A family of doubtful chins forms from the loose flesh under the man's jaw. Then Michael gives him the same line about asking for things in Jesus's name that he fed me.

"What do you think?" Michael says. "Shall we give it a try?"

The man looks to his wife. She pulls down her mouth while raising her eyebrows.

"Why not?" she says.

Michael falls to his knees. He looks up at me and then to the patch of Astroturf beside him. So I fall to my knees, too.

Michael closes his eyes, furrows his brow, and lays his hands on the man's feet. "Jesus, we ask that you heal this man. That you relieve him from this foot pain, from the torment of these cursed arches that are... too high? Or flat?" Michal pauses, opens his eyes, and looks up to the man. "Which is it?"

"They're too flat," he says.

"These bedeviled flat arches be raised in Jesus's name."

This goes on and on. Soon, other guests gather around to watch, some of them using their phones to record whatever it is that we're doing.

Finally, Michael stands and places a benevolent hand on the man's shoulder. "So how do you feel?" he says. "Any better?"

I just know the guy's going to say yes. He has to. Out of obligation alone he has to. Because when a guy dressed like Jesus spends six and a half minutes praying over your feet (I timed it on the watch I'm not supposed to be wearing), you have to say it worked. But when the man tells Michael his feet do feel better, it sounds genuine. Then, to prove it, he marches in place with a proud, high-elbowed gait. His wife beams. The small crowd applauds. Then, when it's just the two of us again, Michael hits me with the smuggest of grins. Which, to me, doesn't look all that Christ-like.

The next day something strange happens. Actually, two strange things. The first is that Stan, the doubtful heretic from "The Good Shepherd," invites me to lunch. The cast hasn't exactly welcomed me into the flock yet, so it's nice when he says that he and some of the others are going off-park and down the road to the Macaroni Grill. But, before I can tell Stan I'll change and meet him in parking, Michael intervenes.

"Thank you, but we've only got time for a quick bite," he says. "The majority of our break will be spent healing the travelers and spreading the word of God."

Stan side-eyes me for a few seconds. "Suit yourself."

"What the hell was that?" I say to Michael.

"Let's not lose focus," he says. "You and I are building something. Working towards a grander goal. Don't be tempted by some casual hobnobberry."

"That's not what—"

"Respect the path that Christ laid out for us," Michael says. "Become a Jesus first. Then, if you want, you can get the apostles."

But I don't want apostles. I just want some friends.

Still, I follow Michael to lunch. That's where the second strange thing happens.

After I place my order and Becca hands me a bowl of the brown wilted lettuce the Last Supper Café calls a Caesar salad, she slips me a note. *Meet me in the whale. Six o'clock,* it says. I'm shocked. I'm overjoyed. My hands tremble as I read it again and again. I completely forget about my food, which Michael misinterprets as both a commitment to my diet and a desire to speed through lunch and continue our healing works.

We return to the courtyard. Michael solicits more guests. He "cures" a man's tennis elbow, "heals" some arthritis, and I suppose the guests go for it. Honestly, I'm too busy thinking about Becca to pay attention. Then something breaks my reverie. In a patch of sunlight, parked between two faux marble columns, I spot a man in a wheelchair. He's rather large and is in one of those wheelchairs you move by blowing into a straw. His white "Jesus Loves Me" T-shirt has gone transparent with sweat and drool. I pray Michael doesn't see him. Pray he doesn't offer to heal him. Just as my panic begins to bloom, Michael's attention is drawn to another man. He's younger than our usual visitors, maybe forty or so. He's limping past some fake shrubs when we approach. He tells Michael that his name is Hershel and that he suffers from pain in his hips and lower back. Michael circles him a few times, surveying him up and down as though this stranger is a piece of merchandise he is thinking about buying.

"Would you mind taking a seat?" Michael says, pointing to a bench. "And now if you'll raise your legs please."

Hershel complies.

"It's just as I thought," Michael says. "One of your legs is longer than the other. It's causing your hips to be out of alignment, which is causing your pain."

And, sure enough, Hershel's left leg is about two inches shorter than his right. Then Michael gives Hershel his Power of Jesus's Name speech. Then he offers to cure him. By making his leg grow.

"Hershel, will you excuse us for a second?" I say. I drag Michael beside a statue of an angel wielding a sword of fire. "What are you doing?"

"I'm helping this visitor. I'm showing him the power of his faith, the power of God's love."

"You can't heal this man."

"The other travelers were healed."

"Yeah, maybe, but those were joint and muscle issues. Internal pain.

Invisible results. This is different. You can't make this guy's leg grow."

Michael smiles and cocks his head to the side. "You're right," he says. "*I* can't heal this man. But Jesus can." Then he returns to Hershel and kneels in front of him. Then he looks over his shoulder to me. "You coming?"

Hershel is still on the bench, looking confused, looking lost, looking like maybe he should have gone to SeaWorld instead. Saying no to Michael, abandoning him, feels like I'd be abandoning Hershel. So what the hell? I kneel beside Michael.

"Hold his legs," he says. Then Michael waves his hands over Hershel's legs and begins praying. "Lord, heal this man, relieve him from this affliction. Left leg grow. Left leg grow. Left leg grow in Jesus's name. Hips be aligned, back pain be healed. In Jesus's name, we ask you." Then Michael pauses and leans down to check if there's been any change, any growth. This process—praying, then checking—continues four more times.

"It usually only takes a few minutes," Michael says to Hershel, and then he turns to me, a perplexed look on his face.

And I, for some reason, allow my face to mirror his mystery, as if I too am baffled by God's unwillingness to cooperate.

Undeterred, Michael continues praying.

Why not right leg shrink, I wonder? Wouldn't that work, too? Aren't we just trying to even this guy out? Maybe that's the problem. Maybe we're being too specific. Maybe God doesn't like being boxed-in, creatively speaking.

Hershel's legs are getting heavy.

Michael's face is uncomfortably close to mine.

My arms are beginning to shake.

Michael's breath smells like Virginia Slims.

I wish I hadn't skipped lunch.

Soon, I notice the courtyard has become a lot more crowded. Visitors are lining up outside the doors of the auditorium. I shift Hershel's legs to one hand so I can check my watch. "The Ultimate Sacrifice" is about to begin.

"Michael. Michael," I say, interrupting his prayer, "it's five 'til. We have to go."

But he doesn't stop. Instead Michael prays faster and louder, as if, this entire time, speed and volume have been the issue.

The doors to the auditorium open.

Guests begin filing in.

"Hey," I say, "we have to leave. Right now."

Michael stops praying and once again leans down to examine Hershel's legs. "There's...yeah, there does seem to be some new growth. They're not totally even just yet, but that left leg is definitely longer."

Hershel stretches his neck to see for himself. But, of course, there's no change, no growth, his legs are as misaligned as they were when we started.

"Sir, I'd love to stay here, continue being a vessel for the Lord's healing influence, and finish you off," Michael says, "but I have to, you know, I gotta go." Then Michael claps Hershel on the thigh, stands, and jogs into the auditorium, leaving me still on my knees, still holding Hershel's legs in my hands.

The interesting thing about the whale is that it's remote. It's in a far corner of the park, just outside of the Daycare, one of the structures in the Stories of The Bible play area. By six o'clock, the park is closing, and the Daycare has been closed for an hour. No one is going to be there. Is that why Becca chose it? For the privacy? Because it's the ideal spot to proclaim one's affections? To perhaps act on those affections?

Here it is, huge and purple, its whale mouth open like the entrance to a small cave, ready to swallow guests.

I breathe into my palm and sniff.

I run my fingers through my hair.

I enter.

Inside is an animatronic Jonah lying on his back, arms and legs flailing in robotic spasms, a look of panic on his face. Beside him is Becca, leaning against the whale's side, legs crossed at the ankle, a look of anger on her face.

"I don't know what the hell you think you're doing," she says, "but it needs to stop. Right now."

Oh. That's what this is. Okay. "I'm sorry," I say. "I don't mean to stare. I just thought that maybe, that first day, we had a kind of a connect—"

"What are you talking about?" she says.

"What are you talking about?"

"The circus sideshow nonsense you and Michael are pulling in the courtyard. What are you thinking?"

"That? That's nothing. Michael's just threatened by Colin. He's worried about being forced out and thinks the healing thing will help."

"He's delusional."

"Yeah."

"And he's dangerous. And he's using you."

I open my mouth to disagree or at least explain why I go along with it, but nothing comes out.

"I suppose Michael's told you all about when he played Jesus in the crucifixion?" Becca says.

He has, in fact. Repeatedly. Apparently, before the Garden of Faith Auditorium was built, "The Ultimate Sacrifice" was performed outside. Guests would gather around a large, concrete hill that was meant to be Calvary. Michael said that his performance of Jesus was so moving that sometimes people would faint. He said that during one particularly powerful performance, five visitors passed out.

"Did he mention that those people passed out during the summer?" Becca says. "Or that, back then, there were no chairs. How long do you think old people can stand in the sun? In Florida? In July? Of course they passed out."

"Michael said it was the power of The Holy Spirit."

"You're an idiot."

I look down at Jonah, lost and confused, thrashing with everything he's got, going nowhere. "What do you want from me?"

Becca steps away from the whale's side, rests her palm on my wrist. "I'm just trying to help," she says. "You seem like a nice and fairly normal guy, which is in short supply around here. Do I think you should keep your distance from Michael? Am I worried he's going to drag you down with him? Yeah."

Her hand feels nice.

"Okay."

The next morning, I'm able to avoid Michael right up until the beginning of "The Good Shepherd." Afterwards, he's still looking for me, so I hide in the men's room. When I finally emerge, I see Michael at the far end of The Jerusalem Market, talking with Ravanel.

I change out of my Bartimaeus costume and find a note stuck to my locker. This one is from Kenny, the stage manager. The note reads: *Cast meeting in the auditorium. 11 a.m.* I check my watch. It's 10:55.

When I enter the auditorium, the house lights are off, but the stage is illuminated. The curtain is up, and all of the props and set dressing have been cleared away. As I make my way across the stage, from somewhere in the darkness comes the sound of a sheep bleating. And then the guttural grunts of a camel. Which is weird.

Kenny enters from stage right. He's followed by Stan and Chelsea and Melanie and some other members of the cast. Behind them, waiting just backstage, I can see Becca. The others form a semicircle in front of me.

Then a low rumble of thunder echoes throughout the auditorium.

This doesn't feel like a cast meeting.

"We have to talk," Kenny says. "There've been a number of visitors who have registered some very serious complaints. They're saying you and Michael are going around claiming you can heal them. Is this true?"

Suddenly, I'm very tired. Tired of notes and secret meetings. I'm tired of the drama of this place. I'm about to tell Kenny everything—about Michael and Colin, Michael's jealousy, and his plan to reclaim the Jesus role—when I see Becca just over his shoulder. She's shaking her head from side to side.

"No," I say. "It wasn't me."

"He's lying," Chelsea yells, stepping forward, her finger aimed at my face. "I've seen you in the courtyard with him. I've seen the two of you kneeling in front of guests, laying hands on them like a couple of lunatics." Chelsea continues yelling about blasphemy and false idols, her face turning red with the exertion. So red in fact that it all but obscures the copious amounts of rouge she insists on wearing. Perhaps, I think, her circulation concerns aren't as bad as she lets on, though this seems like a bad time to mention it.

"Are you listening to me?" she says, and then turns to the group. "He's not even listening to me."

Just as I'm about to respond, the auditorium fills with the sound of a donkey braying. Then trumpets blaring.

"C'mon, guys," Kenny says, shielding his eyes as he looks up into the lights toward the technical booth. "We're trying to have a conversation here."

"Sorry," a voice says over the P.A. system. "Pastor Ravanel wants us to do a run-through of the audio effects. Shouldn't be much longer."

Then there's the sound of a whip cracking. Then a hammer hitting a metal spike.

"Yes," I say, "I was in the courtyard with Michael, but it's not what you think. Honestly, I'm not sure why I was there. I certainly wasn't trying to heal people. I don't even believe in what Michael's doing."

"Pastor Ravanel is taking care of Michael," Kenny says. "I'm here to be sure that you're not also a problem. That you're not with him."

"I'm not. I swear."

"Okay," Kenny says, "that's good enough for me." He turns to the group. "Everyone good? Satisfied?"

Each person nods while mumbling some degree of acceptance.

Then Kenny leaves, followed by the others.

Even Becca has disappeared.

Again, I'm alone on the stage.

Then, from the darkness, from every corner of the auditorium, comes the sound of a rooster crowing.

It's my lunch break when I leave the auditorium, but for some reason, I don't feel like eating. Instead, I just wander around the park, making sure to steer clear of the courtyard. I'm down by the delivery entrance when I run into Michael. His hair is pulled back into a ponytail, and he's wearing jeans and a gray T-shirt. I've never seen him out of costume. It's disorienting. His T-shirt reads, "Not Today Satan."

"Hey," I say, but Michael only nods in response.

We just stare at each other for a few moments, the beeping sound of a truck backing up mercifully breaking the silence.

"It seems I'll be leaving this place sooner than I would have liked," Michael says after the truck has parked.

"I'm sorry."

"It's God's will."

"Yeah, I suppose, but still. When they asked me what we were doing, I didn't know it would lead to this."

"It's fine," Michael says. "Really. You don't have to worry about me."

Then he smiles, and I don't know if he's still in character or if he really means it, but Michael lays a hand upon my shoulder, hits me with those liquid eyes, and says, "I'll be back."

More and Less Human

Okay, gun to your head or malignant tumors on your pancreas, what would you say is the body's best organ? Aesthetically speaking? Perhaps you've never had cause to think about this, to dwell on the artistic appeal of our inner workings. Understandable. Take your time with your answer. I've, apparently, got anywhere from nine to eighteen months. For now, for me, it's the liver. Has been for years. No matter how many other organs I make, the liver holds a special place in my heart. Have you ever seen a liver? It's gorgeous. With its aerodynamic lines, its smooth spaceship curves. The way it gleams with an oxblood sheen. The liver looks sculpted by an advanced race of artisans. Ancient Babylonians believed the liver—not the brain or the heart, but the liver—was the seat of the soul, the source of human spirit and emotion. They also believed the penalty for beating a pregnant woman was ten shekels, but still. It's easy to see how they were swayed.

You know what's not an attractive organ? Maybe the least attractive? The pancreas. It's a fleshy mess, a giant piece of chewed gum whose shape is phallic in nature. It's no wonder the pancreas is stowed behind the stomach, tucked out of sight. In the event of an abdominal incision, it is not one of the organs you want in the welcoming party. There is nothing artistic about the pancreas, nothing that suggests any craftsmanship, any advanced engineering. No one has ever thought the essence of humanity was housed in that cock-shaped chicken cutlet. Perhaps I sound a bit biased, a tad incensed, like I'm being too hard on the pancreas. Perhaps it's because I've recently learned mine is going to kill me.

After the exam room and the examination table whose butcher paper itched the backs of my legs, after the IV of contrast dye and the CT scan, I was told to get dressed, that the doctor would be with me momentarily. It was much longer than momentarily. The doctor took me to her office, sat beside me. She had a fine-boned, narrow face and the gold frames of her glasses were the exact color of her highlights. I don't believe people who regularly dispense terminal diagnoses should have highlights. There are no highlights. She hit me with the news, sat back, crossed her legs. She was wearing Crocs.

"Would you like us to call a loved one?" she said.

"A loved one. Yes please. That sounds nice."

We sat for a second in a new kind of silence.

"Who should we call?"

Who indeed? My folks dead, my distant family distant, no names sprung to mind. "I don't know."

"No? No one?" she said, and somehow, the pained expression on her thin face was worse than when she told me I had cancer.

"There's a woman. You could say...I would say that, yeah, I love her." This just came spilling out, despite it being something I've never admitted to anyone else, something I've barely begun admitting to myself. It's like my mind knew what was coming and was accelerating my comfort with truth, vulnerability. My tolerance to shame. "But she doesn't love me," I said. "Does that still count?"

"I believe it does."

She called Laura.

Now I'm shuffling down a hospital hallway with prescriptions for painkillers, for fatigue, for nausea. Prescriptions for other pills to counter the side-effects from the first batch. I turn the corner and see Laura in the waiting room, absently flipping through a magazine. Laura works in Muscles and this—watching her day after day construct a perfect pair of deltoids or intricately assemble a trapezius, the way she nibbles on one of her long black curls as she layers sheets of fascia, surrounded by all that capillary-rich red—has shaped my perception of her. Though no matter where we worked, her beauty, her elegant animal grace would be just as apparent.

Laura stands when she sees me. "What is it? What's the word?"

"Advanced."

In her car I tell Laura what the doctor told me. That the tucked away location of the pancreas—that biological eyesore—makes early detection difficult. And, because there are few, if any initial symptoms, by the time pancreatic cancer is discovered it's often advanced. While I was blissfully unaware, trudging through the minutia of my day-to-day, my cancer was growing, maturing, blowing right past stages I and II. I long for that lost time.

"I feel like some distant, deadbeat dad," I tell Laura as we stop for a light. "The kind who sees his kids once a year and is shocked at how big they've become. Except instead of them resenting me and rebelling with sex and drugs, they've decided to kill me."

Laura turns, stares at me. She tries smiling but it looks more like a wince. "Most kids find a way to kill their parents," she says. "One way or another."

Laura has a daughter from an early and ultimately failed marriage. Margot makes her living posting pictures of herself in various bras and panties and then selling those infused unmentionables to weirdos on the Internet. I'm ashamed to admit I've checked out her site, but proud to say I've never purchased anything.

We stop at the pharmacy to fill my prescriptions.

"So, home then?" Laura says.

"No. Not yet. Let's go back to work."

"Really?"

"I need something to keep me busy, to keep my mind off my body."

"But the lab? You really think that best place for you, given, you know, everything about it?"

"It will be fine," I say.

"No, it won't."

Laura's right. It's not fine. As soon as we enter the lab, I spot a half-assembled cadaver on a steel gurney. The head and legs are missing, and the chest cavity is open, the perfect, cancer-free organs flaunting beneath the fluorescents. To my right, Cheryl from Skeletons is shaping femurs on a lathe. The whirring when the two make contact is louder than usual, the noise continuing to pinball around my skull even as Cheryl finishes, reaches for a fresh bone. I head for my station, stumble a bit. When I reach out to catch myself, my hand lands on eyes, dozens of eyes fresh from their molds, drying on a giant cookie sheet. The ones that don't go rolling away stare up at me with a portentous knowing.

"Okay," Laura says, grabbing my shoulders, steadying me. "Let's find you a seat."

She steers me through the MOV lab, past Vascular and Organs, to her station in Muscles. At her desk is a recently completed pectoralis major floating in a shallow hydration tray. I sit and hold my head in my hands even as I feel it drifting toward the tray, toward the wet, cushion-soft muscle. It feels nice.

You may have heard that fewer and fewer people are donating their bodies to science. Sure, people still go in for the philanthropic ego puff from organ donation, but donor numbers for surgical testing and education have fallen in recent years. It seems surviving relatives are no longer willing to offer their loved ones as fodder for the anatomy labs. The thoughts of their mothers or fathers, their sweet Bubby with her house gown and occasional racism, being hacked to pieces by inquisitive medical students is too much to bear.

When I first started working here, Dr. Haldane and his team of doctors, engineers, and artisans were already on the forefront of creating synthetic tissue that mimics the mechanical and physiological properties of the human body. Now our synthetic humans (synmans) are the most intricately assembled and accurate representation of the human anatomy ever devised. If that last part sounds like corporate copy, it's because it is. Dr. Haldane wrote it. He oversees every detail of our operation. That tray of eyeballs I tumbled into, all the irises have this river rock shade of gray. Every synman has them. The fact that they are the exact shade of gray as Dr. Haldane's eyes is something we all know but don't really discuss. Even so, Haldane's a nice enough guy. A bit of a narcissist but what creator isn't?

Dr. Haldane likes to say that though the initial goal was cadaver replication and replacement, we have long surpassed it. Our surgical simulators and other products are now far superior. We are now better than the dead.

That last part of his speech usually gets some looks.

Even before donations flatlined, cadavers for surgical practice were woefully ineffective. Any of the risks, the potential mistakes and occasions to quell the rising tide of panic and display a doctorly calm were rendered moot by the fact that the patient was, you know, dead.

Our latest models come equipped with a small motor in the heart and a complete vascular network, allowing for a fully functioning circulatory system. That means they bleed. That means if you're a resident performing a routine inguinal hernia surgery and, oopsie doopsie, you nick the iliac artery, the synman will hemorrhage, its abdominal cavity rapidly filling with blood. Another implant syncs to an EKG machine, making the alarm sound and the monitor display the spiking, violent V's of imminent death. Cadavers can't do that. You can't kill what's already dead.

It's decided that I should take some time off, use it to process my disease and plan accordingly. My first round of chemo isn't for a couple of days, so now I'm watching TV and eating painkillers. I'm also replaying the whole "no loved ones" scene with the doctor. It bothers me. Not as much as the diagnosis, but this is where my focus is. Maybe I'm compartmentalizing, avoiding the larger issues. Maybe there's only so much we can handle at once. I might be lacking some loved ones now, but I'm sure I've loved in the past, put myself out there, received and returned the required affections. I'm pretty sure. I've definitely leered and longed for. I spent my high school years huffing the fantasy-fuel of unattainable things. Chiefly among them, Emma Ramsbottom.

As one of humanity's genetic jackpot winners, Emma enslaved my senses. The silken sunshine of her hair. The rhythm of her ass—heart-shaped and heaven-sent, nothing ram-like about it—as she walked, how those denim undulations conducted the flutter of my pulse. But words fails. Perhaps it's enough to know that her surname—it's potential for social stigma, the low-hanging orchard of ridicule it would normally inspire—was never wielded against her. Emma was that beautiful.

College proved kinder, the women more approachable, less particular. Booze helped. Senior year I met Debbie Eaton. After the poke and prattle of third date fondue, Debs agreed to come over, have a drink, spend the night. She moved in a few months later.

Things were good until they weren't. For a few years we shared kind words, kinder acts. Cuddles on the couch. Just after she moved in, Debbie bought us a couch. Perhaps it was her nod to nesting, to domestic coupling. It may have also been that, prior to her purchase, my living room furniture consisted of two lawn chairs I had found behind the laundry room.

Towards the end of our relationship, the beginning of our unraveling, Debbie took to the tub. I'd come home to find her in the bathroom, in the tub, knees to her chest, arms wrapped around her knees. Though it was clear Debbie had been crying, there was never any water in the tub. She was fully clothed. The whole thing was a bit of theater, a piece of performance art. I knew her tears were the byproduct of my staying out later and later with friends, my inability to answer or return calls. But I never understood the point of her crying *in* the tub, its symbolism. I still don't. Was it that I always arrived home too soon, spoiling her plans to fill the tub with her tears, to amass and showcase her sadness by the gallon? Maybe I would have understood the tub's meaning if I had searched my soul, looked down deep. I've never had much of a down deep.

I take full responsibility for what happened with Debbie, our eventual uncoupling. But I also blame boredom, tedium, being tasked to maintain love when we were swaddled in comfort, bubble wrapped in monotony. It's the unfairness of our era. Where are our external threats, our existential crises? What hostile actions or unimaginable forces are there to realign our perspective, to stoke the relationship fires and keep those longing logs burning late into the night? No couple needed a "date night" to spice things up as lava poured through the streets of Pompeii. There were no obligatory rubs and tugs as the S.S. were goose-stepping beneath the Arc de Triomphe. I needed the benefit of a brink, an opportunity to sharpen my priorities on the edge of the abyss.

I tried explaining all of this to Debbie during one of her tub nights, but she just looked up at me, blinking muddily through mascara tears. I guess Debs disagreed. Maybe she didn't understand. Maybe she didn't hear me. The acoustics in that bathroom were never any good.

On the eve of her departure I panicked at the thought of her leaving. I feared change, loneliness. I also wasn't too thrilled about having to pay her half of the rent. I wrote Debbie a desperate, pleading missive. I bared my soul, begged her to reconsider, to stay. I wrote it on Post-Its and stuck all four on the wall by the front door. When I got home that night Debbie was gone, her things were gone, the Post-Its had come unstuck. They laid curled on the carpet.

Now Debs is long gone. Her sofa is still here. I imagine Debbie wanted to make a hasty escape and the sofa is heavy. It's a sleeper.

I suppose I've got my brink now, a front row seat to my own private abyss. But now, like this, who would want me? Maybe it's time to make amends. I find my phone, plop back down on the couch and give Debbie a call.

"Deborah Standish," she says after a few rings.

In the background are the high-pitched squeals of children. I've heard through the various digital grapevines that Debbie had married, made some people. "Hiya, Debs. It's me."

"Oh."

It's funny, but her "oh" has the same steeled, doom-drenched inflection mine did when I was told I was dying of cancer.

"How are things?"

"Is this some kind of friendly call?"

"Am I not being friendly? I thought I'd say hi, catch up. Do some catching up from our couch."

"Our what?"

"The couch. Our couch. I still have it. I'm sitting on it now."

"Oh," she says again. This time her tone is more three-legged dog, little girl with a harelip.

I tell Debbie about my diagnosis, the treatment plans and procedures, the likelihood of them being anything but futile.

"Well, I hope you get what you deserve."

"Why would you say that?"

Debbie sighs heavily into the phone. It brings me back.

"What exactly can I do for you?" she says.

"Nothing. It's, you know, with everything that's happening I've had an occasion to pause, to reflect. To regret the missteps, the bumblings, the—"

"Selfishness and narcissism and outright asshole behavior?"

"Those too. Definitely all of that. It's just, afterwards, when I'm gone, I don't want you to think poorly of me."

"I don't think of you."

A few hours later, I'm adrift on a sea of prescribed delirium when there is a knock on the door. I open it to find a moon-faced young man sporting a set of round rosy cheeks and a cascading brown beard. He looks like his mother had dalliances with a garden gnome.

"Good afternoon, sir. I'm here to inform you I am a convicted sexual offender."

Part of me—most of me—is relieved he's not here to sell magazines or talk about Jesus.

He introduces himself as Porter Fisher, says he's going door-to-door as part of new community notification program. "It's an amendment to Megan's Law," he says.

"Megan? Is that the name of the girl you...diddled? I'm not familiar with the nomenclature."

"I never assaulted any girls?"

"Oh. Boys then. Well, I suppose the heart wants what it wants."

Porter looks at me like he's just stepped in dog shit. "No. No boys either."

"I'm confused."

"One night I decided to walk home after last call. Walk, mind you, because I thought I'd had too much to drive. I cut through a park, some playground, stopped to take a leak. A cop was parked across the street, hit me with his search light. Caught me mid-stream. Got me for indecent exposure, lewd and lascivious behavior. Those charges, when they occur in a park or any place where children may likely frolic, regardless of the time of day, come with a lifetime brand as a sexual offender and a spot on the registry."

"No shit," I say.

"On the contrary, sir. It's nothing but shit. Mountains of it."

"I have terminal cancer.

"That's also not good."

We stand there for a while, listen to birds squawk at one another.

"You a drinking man, Porter?"

"I've spent all afternoon telling strangers I'm a child molester when I am not. What do you think?"

"I've got pills, too."

I must doze off for a bit. When I wake up I see an emaciated polar bear. It's trudging through what's left of the tundra.

"I love these things," Porter says from his end of the couch.

"Polar bears?"

"Nature documentaries."

I watch the polar bear and wonder about my remaining days, how to best spend the time I have left. I know I should do something big, something from my bucket list now that its kicking is imminent. Timing is a concern. I'd happily blow through my savings if they could give me an exact date of demise. But that's not how it works. They tell you to make every moment count, to live each day as if it's your last, but they also expect you to squirrel something away in the event you don't die. *Carpe diem*, but budget accordingly. I wonder if there is some sort of charitable support, a middle-aged man Make-A-Wish.

I imagine the Make-A-Wish man, his casual Friday khakis, the overly-gelled hair he parts on the side. "If you could have anything," he says, "what would it be? Anything at all. Other than not dying of course." Then he smiles, winks.

But what would I want? My mind immediately runs to the extravagant, the obscene, some id-driven debauchery. Perhaps the Oprah suite, a trail mix of pharmaceutical-grade uppers and hallucinogens, a cadre of top shelf prostitutes. But something exotic, off menu. Ginger Asians with Australian accents. For a while we'd have our fun, our fondles and cavorts. But soon concerns would creep in. The transactional nature of prostitution has always failed to inoculate me against insecurity, my ever-present need to please. My stamina would dwindle. I'd realize I'd bit off more than I could satisfy. That my eyes were bigger than my... you get it. The girls would grow bored, I'd get angry. There'd be yelling, tears, a stormy roar. The girls would gather their things in a rush, high heels looped through their fingers, make a bare-footed departure. Then one of them—the kindest maybe—would pause in the doorway, turn to me. "G'day," she'd say.

Now, as the polar bear tromps after a trash bag enlivened by arctic winds, I feel a small spark of pain at the base of my back. With each breath I take the flame grows, surging up my spine. Waves of nausea hit me, doubling me over as I lurch to the bathroom. The mechanics of lifting the toilet lid prove to be too much and I puke in the tub. Afterwards, with my cheek against the cool porcelain and a film of spit and vomit on my lips, I realize my days of independence, maybe autonomy, are numbered. I'm going to need help. There's only so many people to whom you can fully surrender your ego, wave the white flag to pride and embrace shame like a lover. Those people are usually loved ones, but I'm a bit light on those at the moment. Maybe all this terminal muss and fuss will be easier with a stranger.

Porter looks up when I return to the living room.

"How would you like to make some extra money?"

It turns out it's hard to find steady work when your name is added to the list of toddler-touchers. Whether or not you actually touched any toddlers seems to be beside the point. So, on Monday, Porter drives me to chemo. The treatment facility is steel and smoked glass comprised of high, hopeful angles. As we enter, the doors part with a nearly silent *swish*.

My oncologist is an unseasonably tan man in black scrubs. His hair is a swoopy dollop of dark brown, but he also has a set of long white sideburns, like a pair of frosted Floridas. I'm trying to decide if he dyes his hair or bleaches his sideburns when I realize he's started speaking.

"...with the hope of turning your terminal disease into a chronic illness."

"That sounds like a rough compromise," I say.

"I'm afraid rough compromises are where we are. If you respond well to the chemo, if we can keep the tumors localized to the head of your pancreas, you may be eligible for what's called a Whipple procedure. We'll go in and attempt to remove the tumors, but to do so we have to rearrange most of your abdominal organs. You should know it's an extremely complex operation."

"Oh, you don't have to tell me. I've seen my share of people get assembled."

He crinkles up his brown brow.

"Not people, per se. I build synthetic cadavers."

"Okay."

"They're better than the dead."

"How nice for them."

We stare at each other for a second. The air conditioner kicks on.

"I know this is a lot to absorb," the doctor says. "Sometimes, as a means of defense, the mind reels, goes spiraling off in random directions. It's perfectly normal."

I decide he must be dying his hair. The sideburns are his natural color. "I don't think I'm doing that."

"Okay then. Let's get started."

In the infusion center I'm seated in an overstuffed recliner, it's vinyl shiny, stain-resistant. Across from me are two other occupants, both garlanded with IV lines. We do the toothless smiles, the head nods. Then I lean back and wait for my cautious portion of poison.

There's something about being surrounded by disease and decimation, the various measures to halt death, that makes you appreciate being healthy, alive. It makes me want to stick around, to experience life's varied offerings. I even find myself nostalgic for the bitter fruit of social failures. How many more times, in some wayward attempt to woo a stranger, will I stick my foot in my mouth? How many more times will my head enjoy the warm cozy myopia of my ass? I want to stay here, even if that means being mired in the absurd and awkward and awful. I want to live.

Good news. The chemo must be working, must be killing my tumors, because every part of me feels like it's dying. For the third time today I'm humped before the toilet, in between bouts of nausea. It's a respite from the bucks and shudders, the hot tears, the strands of spit and bile. Porter stands beside me. I can sense the weight of his wavering hand, his tentative attempt to comfort.

"It's okay," I say. "You can touch me. I'm not a little kid."

"I never touched any kids!"

"I know, buddy. I know." I turn, smile up at him.

Then I puke on his shoes.

Later, I send Porter out for supplies, sundries, things I can hopefully keep down. I throw in some new shoe money. Porter returns with broths, teas, fruits that are easily stewed, mashed. He holds up a half-gallon jug of some sports drink. "It's got electrolytes," he says. From another bag, Porter produces a plastic beach bucket, a bottle of toilet cleaner. "When you get sick you don't always make it to the bathroom in time."

"I'm aware."

"And even when you do make it, you don't always get all of it in the bowl."

"Thank you."

I notice the toilet cleaner is the exact same shade of chemical blue as my sports drink. No wonder I have fucking cancer.

A few days later I'm home, fresh from a recent round of chemo. I'm on the couch, trying to get comfortable, trying to nap. Each flip and shift releases rancid pockets of air. I'm still aware of my aroma, the sour stench of my decay. That I'm still able to differentiate, that I'm not yet so consumed by this disease, makes me feel healthier than I am.

The mirrors have turned against me, though. They were never what I'd call an ally, but with particular angles and flattering lighting and a touch of delusion I could usually cobble together enough confidence to face the world. Not now. Now mirrors are shotgun blasts of truth. They reflect only my rot. I can no longer bear bearing witness to my wilt. I've asked Porter to remove them, cover them. Call it vanity, but the truth is I'd rather not know. I'm backing away from the brink, choosing to cling to the bits of ignorant bliss I have left.

I call Laura. "Hey, I need to get out of here. Come get me. I've packed a picnic."

"A picnic? I don't know. My day is sort of swamped."

"You can't turn me down. I'm a dying man."

"How long do you think you get to play that card?"

"Until I'm dead."

"Fine. I'll be there in twenty minutes."

"Make it thirty. I could use a shower."

Around an hour later I tell Laura to turn down Venus Drive. We pull up to a modest brick home. The roof is long gone, the house and yard in late stages of nature consumption, reclamation. The August I turned thirteen, Hurricane Andrew tore across southern Florida. While my parents and I evacuated inland, spent the night huddled up in a Howard Johnson's, Andrew was ripping the roof off our house. Four days later we were allowed to return home. We collected the things least bloated with rainwater and rot. We collected the insurance money and never looked back.

"What are we doing here?" Laura says.

"Looking back."

We climb the steps to the listing porch, the wooden railings rotted away, the steps velveted in moss. Leaves and twigs and loose bricks litter what used to be the foyer. Ivy insists itself though the living room's broken windows, crawls along the walls. I peek in the kitchen. The space between the stove and the breakfast bar is now a small forest of saplings that have burst through the warped linoleum. I look to Laura.

I want to say something profound, something about the tenacity of nature, its overwhelming effort to exist despite the odds, to endure. How the whole spectacle should be inspiring but isn't. She catches me staring.

"Wanna see my old room?"

I find a spot relatively clear of debris, hand Laura the picnic basket, spread out the blanket. I look around my roofless room. Even though the air carries unmistakable top-notes of hobo urine, and on the wall where my Bo Jackson poster used to hang someone's graffiti suggests Staci's affinity for fellatio, the lighting in here is much improved. I envy the house's graceful deterioration, the odd beauty of it.

"Did you know it takes less than forty-eight hours for the body to undergo complete rigor mortis?" I say. "After less than a week, the body's enzymes and bacteria have eaten it from within. The skin slips off. Organs liquify and leak out of various orify. Or is it orifices? I feel like I should know this."

Laura looks at me for what feels like a long time. "Your picnic banter needs work."

"Yeah. Sorry."

"What's all this decay talk anyway? The treatments are working, right?"

"I suppose. I don't know."

A lizard crawls along a collapsed pipe.

"So, you wanna fool around?" I say.

"Excuse me?"

"My transitions are also lacking. You may not believe it, but you're the first girl—woman—I've had in here."

"I believe it."

"So what do you say? How about a little sympathy sex? Some conciliatory coitus? You can be my middle-aged-man Make-A-Wish."

"What?"

"Nothing. Forget it."

Laura smiles, places a hand near my leg. Not on it, but near it. "Maybe some other time."

"Some other time? There is no other time. This is it. This is me in peak condition. You won't want me later, not when I'm shitting myself as drool spills from my slack jaw."

"Probably not, though you've been drooling over me for years."

"That's true, I have. I didn't think you knew."

"You haven't been exactly subtle."

"You know, sometimes I drool over you while I'm on the toilet, so it's like we're almost there anyway."

"Jesus Christ. Comments like that will make me start rooting for the cancer."

"That's my girl."

Laura tenses, winces with the association. She slides her hand away. "Yeah, well, this girl is starving. She reaches for the picnic basket, lifts the lid. "Is it just beer in here?"

"Give me one, will you?"

The next day Porter and I are parked in front of the TV. He's half-way through a six pack, I'm cuddled up in a soft opiate cocoon. We're watching another nature documentary. It's seems that for every creature walking or flying or swimming along the planet, most of life is spent searching for food and avoiding death and somewhere in between trying to have some sex. I suppose it's that way for us too, but with stuff, things, the bills for those things.

Now we're in the rainforest watching one of those birds of paradise, its mating ritual. He's painstakingly clearing a patch of jungle floor, hopping around, beaking away every bit of twig and leaf. Then, free of any foliaged interference, he puffs out his throat, turns it a brilliant bioluminescent teal, hoping a female will notice.

"Ugh," I say. "That's so much work for sex. If I was a bird I'd never get laid."

"You don't get laid now."

"And I can't fly."

Porter drains his beer, stands. "I gotta go. More community notifications."

"The shame parade continues."

"Not how I'd phrase it, but yes."

"Can I come along?"

"Really?"

"Why not? It will give me a chance to meet my neighbors."

"You don't know your neighbors?"

"Does anyone? Plus, it could be fun."

"I doubt it."

"We'll see."

The first door we knock on is answered by a small Italian-looking woman. She has a bulb of black hair streaked with gray, olive skin filigreed by time. Porter hits her with his sexual offender spiel. She says something in an old-world tongue, spits at our feet.

"No, no, no," I say, stepping between them. "You don't understand. He never actually molested any children, not really."

"No?" the woman says, her features softening.

"Nope. But only because he refers to it as 'making love'."

"Dude!" Porter says. "Not cool."

The woman looks from me to Porter, her eyes wide, her tendons taut, the neck cords of outrage.

"I'm just kidding," I say. "He never touched any kids."

"What?" she says. "Then what the hell is this? What the hell is your problem?"

"I'm dying."

You'd think the ability to still find the funny while facing death would be appreciated, admired. But no. Porter refuses to answer or return my calls. Because he can't take a joke I have to take a taxi to my next treatment. When I arrive, instead of being taken to the infusion center, I'm asked to wait in the lobby. So I wait. The receptionist says the doctor would like to speak with me. She leads me back to his office. He still has the tan, the two-toned hair.

"I'm afraid your tumors have become distant," he says.

"Well, it's not like I ever thought of them as cuddly or approachable. More like angst-ridden teenagers lying on their bedroom floors, listening to some godawful, death-metal music, angry at their parents."

The doctor narrows his eyes and brings a fist to his head, right where the brown meets the white. "It means the chemo has been ineffective. Your tumors have spread to other organs, other parts of your body. It's called metastasis."

"Sounds like the name of the band my distant tumors listen to."

"You're not taking this news too seriously."

"I'm taking it the best way I can."

I wander around for a while, find myself on a street flanked by empty storefronts. FOR SALE signs hang in almost every shop window, the phone numbers of hopeful sellers sun-bleached beyond legibility. There's a bar on the corner. The place is empty save the bartender, a little potato of a man who's slumped on a stool, asleep, his legs dangling.

"Excuse me," I say, and then again, a bit louder.

Nothing.

I take out my pill bottle, rattle the pills near his face. He startles awake, almost slides off the stool.

"You got a death wish, fuckface?"

"Whether I do or not is no longer relevant."

"What?"

"May I have a drink please?"

The "please" helps. Not only does the potato pour like an angel, but when I plop my pills into my drink like so many tiny antacids, he doesn't say a word. At some point, after a few rounds, I must have asked him to call me a cab. Though now, I'm having hazy recollections of me just slur-shouting "cab" at him over and over.

Either way there's a car outside.

"Where to?" the guys says as I slide across the vinyl.

We pull up to the front of the lab, but when it takes me thirty, forty fumbling seconds to figure out how to open the door, I decide around back would be better. It's where we keep Shipping. It's where I find Darren packing up a shipment of pediatric intubation trainers. Picture the head and upper chest of a newborn. Now rows and rows of them. Their eyes are scrunched shut, their mouths open as if in the middle of a silent scream.

"It looks like they're crying," I say.

"What's that?"

I point to the units. "Do you think they're crying because they know I'm going to die?"

"What's that?"

I wander past Assembly, stagger into Hydration. The synmans, their various parts, must stay hydrated until they're vacuum-sealed and shipped off to hospitals, universities. Most of the tubs contain complete synmans, fully submerged, staring dead-eyed through the water like drowning victims. The tub on the end is used for miscellaneous parts, pieces. I spot some kidneys, a set of lungs, a complete left arm lying like a log along the bottom. Then I see it, a pinkish, tuberous mass. I reach down, fetch it out. The pancreas is slick in my hand, limp, like some fish washed up on the shore. It's still disgusting, a monstrosity, but also, undoubtedly, better looking than mine.

I want to rip it apart, throw the pieces across the room, screaming as I do so. But I don't. I don't have the drive, the strength. I toss it back in the tub. I imagine the, *if you can't beat them, join them* approach is easier, freeing. I'll bet it's definitely more refreshing. I strip, ease myself into the tub. The water's just cold enough to give me that initial shock, to suck the breath from my lungs before my body numbs, adjusts. A gallbladder bobs to the surface, glances my shoulder. Other parts bump against me like so many bath toys. They remind me of my favorite as a kid, Tub-Time Spiderman. He had red suction cups at the ends of his hands and feet so he could stick to the tiles, dangle above the sudsy depths. I miss that toy. I miss being that little boy who didn't have cancer.

Seconds pass, minutes maybe. I may have taken a quick tub-nap. Also, the water seems to have assumed a viscous quality, a subtle thickening. It's as if I'm no longer submerged but suspended. It could just as easily be the booze, the pills.

Oh, Debbie. Debbie. Debbie. I think, now, I finally understand your retreats to the tub, its womb-like appeal. Perhaps I would have then if you'd only filled it first. If you'd had cancer.

I look up, find Laura looming over me.

"What are you doing?"

"I'm the little boy who has cancer."

I wake up in my bed. The sheets are damp and my pant legs are cinched around my waist. I find some dry clothes. I find Laura in the living room.

"I'm not sure if I owe you a thank you or an apology," I say.

"Both would work."

Laura tells me my ascent from the tub was, unfortunately, less Aphrodite and more of a prolonged and complicated birth. There were periods of resistance, threatening pleas, tears. And that was just me.

"You got to see me naked though. Huh? That's something."

"It was definitely something," she says.

"Thank you for taking care of me. Again."

Laura smiles, shrugs. "I'm running a tab."

"Don't wait too long to collect." I sit beside her. "Look, I know that last few times we've gotten together the circumstances were less than ideal. But I liked having you around. I had fun. More fun than I've had in a while, with anyone. And I don't know if you did too, but maybe if you did we could—"

Laura grabs my hand with both of hers, which shuts me right up.

"Please," she says. "I can't imagine what you're going through and I'm happy to help when I can, but as your friend. Beyond that, I'm just not in a place where I can right now. I'm so sorry."

"It's okay. I understand," I say, choking back a sudden sob. "I'm not sure I can right now with me either."

It takes four more phone calls before Porter agrees to come over, to consider accepting my apology. Telling him I'm dying, definitely this time, may have helped too.

"I'm not very good with people," I say when he takes a seat on the couch.

"Well, I suppose if you were you wouldn't need to pay a stranger to take care of you."

It's an airtight truth, cold, hurtful, but that kind usually is.

Then Porter reaches into his backpack and pulls out a gun. Part of my *mea culpa* was agreeing to buy his revolver. To pay, I'll have you know, considerably more than it is worth. You may think that, as a branded playground predator, Porter has been forced to surrender his right to bear arms. But no, not the case. Such is the bewildering girth of America's freedoms. He's just short on cash, is selling some stuff. I figure the gun could come in handy. You can't be too careful. Death lurks around every corner.

"So are we good?" I say. "You forgive me?"

"I suppose so."

"Great. Because I need a favor."

This time, this time of night, I have Porter park up front. I use my keys, my pass card, head right for Hydration. But Porter lags, lingers. He's standing before a set of metal shelves containing our collection of cast-offs, our misfits, the disfigured fruits of our imaginations. Any synman part or piece that fails inspection is saved, stored. During our downtime we're encouraged to reimagine these pieces, to create sculptures or creatures. Dr. Haldane values the artistic outlet, the comradery. He holds a contest in the spring. I don't mind sharing that last year, my cycloptic, eight-legged spider-baby took home the gold.

"What the hell is this place?" Porter says.

"It's fine. I work here. Worked. C'mon."

We stand at each end of one of the tubs.

"Grab his feet," I say.

"Hey, man. I don't think I can be doing this. I've got priors."

"Don't worry, it's an adult model."

"You're an asshole."

"It'll be fine. I told you, I work here."

"Still, I can't be seen stealing a naked, whatever this thing is."

I lay some cash on the counter, a credit card. I find a lab coat. "Happy now?"

"Ecstatic."

On the terminal timeline, evolution is accelerated. I am not the man I was yesterday. Yesterday I was lost, disillusioned. Yam-brained by booze and pills, I sought the path of least resistance, of acceptance.

But that was yesterday.

Today, tonight, I feel like destroying something.

Porter and I slide the synman in the backseat. We drive out of town, past dying malls, shuttered mills. As the buildings give way to fields and marsh we hook down a dirt road. The three of us bounce along the ruts. Porter hits the high beams and I spot a copse of trees.

"Over there," I say.

In the halogen wash of Porter's headlights we wrestle the synman toward tree, lean him against the trunk.

Then I get the gun.

"Go ahead," I say, handing it to Porter. "Do the honors."

"What? You sure?"

"Of course. Unload your angst. My gift to you."

Porter looks over each shoulder as if there is anyone watching, as if there is anything to see. Then he raises the gun, fires round after round into the synman.

"Oh my God," he says as the boom dies down. "That was awesome."

It doesn't take long before crimson dots bloom large on the lab coat while other, uncovered holes leak rivulets of red.

"What the hell?" Porter puts the gun on the hood, ambles over to the synman as I reload. "This thing bleeds?" he says, tentatively fingering an entry point. "Oh, that's too much, man. You should have told me that."

Porter turns to me just as I put the gun to my head.

I believe I hear him scream, *NO!*

I like to think so.

The Yellow Mama Experience

Mondays mean dusting and windows, so I grab the Windex and the microfiber cloth Professor Orbach insists upon and get to work. I clean the glass dome covering the mummified lynx skull. I dust the bottles of Frigid Jr.'s Concentrated Embalming Fluid. I wipe away the supposed fingerprints from the various display cases—the Ecuadorian shrunken heads, the calcified fetuses, and Charlotte, the eight-legged lamb. Professor Orbach named her after the E.B. White character because of her arachnid resemblance. The professor also appreciates a good literary reference. I've repeatedly listened to her bemoan the decline of pedagogy, how schools like Saint Bart's are filling the minds of girls like me with fear and myopia, denying us the ability to think critically or independently, dooming us to a life where we're only good for keeping our mouths shut and our legs opened.

"Well, it's a Catholic school," I told her, "so that may not exactly be their plan."

"Oh, it is," she said. "They just want you to feel guilty about it, too."

I say "supposed" fingerprints because, in reality, the glass is spotless. There are no fingerprints because no one touches the exhibits because no one comes in here. Though The Spectacularium has been open almost three months, people have been reluctant to "appreciate the unusual and unknown" as the sign suggests.

I once asked the professor about the futility of this chore, why we (I) bothered cleaning already clean exhibits nobody was coming to see in the first place. She looked askance at me, laid a bejeweled hand on my shoulder, and said, "One cannot conduct their life based on the expectations of others. Would you only wash and condition your hair if you thought a young man might run his fingers through it?"

I wanted to tell her that no man, young or otherwise, has ever deigned to run his fingers through the chaotic cloud of orange frizz that is my hair. Instead, I shook my head.

So I keep cleaning. Charlotte's in a three-by-five-foot case, and I squat down so we're eye to glass eye. If I let my focus shift, I can see beyond her downy white fur and find my reflection in the glass. I can see my gut rolls, only slightly exaggerated by my slumped position. I can see my round, ruddy head that Lexie Curlew once described as a jack-o-lantern without the candle, much to the delight of the cafeteria crowd. I focus back to Charlotte and the perpetual frown on her little face. Perhaps the taxidermist formed this expression to evoke some emotional response in the viewer, the same way they make wolves forever snarl. But me, I like to think the look is natural. That it's the result of Charlotte taking in her malformed body and realizing that life is cruel and unfair and would be a series of escalating hardships.

The bell over the front door dings, and I know it's the professor without turning around. She is preceded by her perfume—a heady concoction of jasmine and lavender. It's like having your head dunked into a box of flowers. The professor is wearing one of her seemingly limitless tailored black dresses, this one sleeveless, showcasing a pair of slender yet muscular arms. They amplify my sinew envy.

Professor Orbach stares down at me over the top of her sunglasses. Her steel-colored hair is monumentally piled, as if to suggest its indifference to weather or gravity or any of the challenges faced by mere mortals. "Must you project your grief on that poor creature?" she says. "Hasn't she suffered enough?"

I feign a look of shock and scramble for a response, but the professor doesn't give me the opportunity.

"Besides," she continues, "you and I have a busy day. You-know-what will be delivered in a few hours, and we must make preparations. I must find *the* perfect place." Then off she goes, wandering around The Spectacularium, reorganizing it in her mind, searching for the ideal spot to display our newest exhibit, the one that will change everything.

There have been other exhibits, other saving graces believed to slow, and perhaps even reverse, the steady decline in business. When we first opened, novelty and curiosity got the better of our cautious and generally conservative townspeople. But when they came in and saw the exhibits—the anatomical synthetic model showing the skeletal system, veins, arteries, and organs of a small child, the variety of nineteenth-century planchettes and spiritscopes used to "communicate with the dead," the professor's extensive collection of genetically malformed giraffe skulls—something happened. Pinched faces of concern and confusion, whispers, and sidelong glances from the exhibits to the professor seemed to fill the shop. A few people barely made it past the doorway before taking in the main room, huffing audibly, and then turning around and walking out. I wasn't surprised. Our town has never exactly embraced eclecticism. Mere mentions of diversity and multiculturalism have been historically countered with sallow concerns about community and identity. Even when the Christian-themed Chinese restaurant opened a few years ago, it was only able to slide past any initial xenophobia on the enduring appeal of Jesus. And even with that, when the restaurant was forced to close—rumors spanned from a child pornography ring to the late owner leaving all of his money to a mistress in Florida—more than a few people were quick to link the immoral, lascivious behavior to ethnic food. When the professor opened The Spectacularium, she unknowingly gave the town somewhere new to focus its fears.

By the end of that first week, everyone had an opinion, and none of them were flattering. The professor was deemed a witch, or a cultist, or a Satan worshipper. Others were convinced she was a criminal of some variety—a smuggler perhaps, if not some kind of serial killer. *Where does she get all of those bones? And those fetuses!* The professor felt that the accusations from some small-minded, small-townspeople didn't warrant a response. She may have been right, but the problem with not defending yourself is that people can—and do—say whatever they want. And even when you do defend yourself, people, namely Lexie and the rest of Saint Bart's prancing ponies, still say whatever they want. But you've got to try.

The best we could do on short notice was a "reporter" for the Sunday circular Father Delaney hands out after Mass. So that Monday afternoon, someone's grandmother, squat and stoop-shouldered, walked in wearing a gray pantsuit with pink polka dots. She didn't introduce herself, just fished a pad from her giant purse and toddled through the shop scribbling notes between outbursts of *Well well* and *Oh my.*

We watched her from behind the counter, the professor fingering the stem of her champagne flute. Earlier that day, Professor Orbach sent me out for Prosecco and peach puree stating, "The ability to craft a perfect Bellini is the cornerstone of any civilized existence."

"May we help you?" the professor finally asked.

The woman turned. "Perhaps. Can you explain to my readers and me why you've chosen to infect our town with this morbidity and indecency?"

The professor smiled, took a sip of her drink, and then returned it to the counter, where it sat luminous in the sunlight slicing through the windows. "So much for unbiased journalism," the professor said to me. "And to think, I expected more from the...what was it?"

"Saint Bartholomew's Gazette," I said.

"As to your question, Ms.—"

"Scunthorpe."

"I'm sure you can agree that terms like *morbid* and *indecent* are subjective in nature. What one person may find indecent, another may think perfectly appropriate to, say, wear when conducting an interview."

Scunthorpe pursed her already wizened lips. They looked like one of her polka dots.

The two women continued to spar. The professor argued for the insight and historical value of her artifacts, the education and perspective they were bringing to "a town in dire need of both." Ms. Scunthorpe countered, calling The Spectacularium an "off-season haunted house" trafficking in "shock value and grotesquery." The entire time I held my head in my hands, weary at the thought of having to find another after-school job.

At some point, Ms. Scunthorpe pivoted to the recent gossip, namely the accusations that the professor was a cultist or Satan worshipper.

"I'll have you know I am a Christian. As a matter of fact, I've read the Bible at least four times," the professor confessed. And then to me said, "For a time, I was in possession of one of the remaining complete Gutenberg's. What a beautiful book that was."

But I was staring at Scunthorpe. Her indignation had stalled out, and confusion was manifesting on her face in furrows and grimaces.

"You?" she said, gesturing toward the professor who was busy topping off her drink with more Prosecco. "You read the Good Book?"

"I do. I skip over the hateful or misogynistic or outright ridiculous parts. Naturally. You should try it. Makes for a quick read."

That pretty much concluded the interview. Scunthorpe scuttled off in a huff, and by that Sunday the circular had, well, circled, confirming what the town had suspected from the beginning.

Business suffered. There were some dark and despondent days. There was a day I found the professor in her office, listless with despair on the long tongue of her oxblood chaise, halfway through a bottle of Bodega Catena Zapata. "Mendoza Malbecs are the only reds worth imbibing," she said, aiming her empty wine glass at me as if it were a gun. "Everything else is a perversion of the palette. Don't let any of your little friends try to convince you otherwise."

"I eat lunch alone," I told her. "In the gym, on top of the rolled up wresting mats, and not even the ones by the door, but the other, older ones in the far corner of the gym."

"What does that have to do with anything?"

A few hours later, undoubtedly inspired by her Argentinian wine, Professor Orbach stormed out of her office, waving a piece of paper in my face. On it were ideas for new exhibits, exhibits guaranteed to bring in customers.

The first was her "Female Oppression Throughout the Ages" exhibit. The professor was hoping to woo some of the Women's Studies majors from the community college, and it worked, for a while. The shop saw the occasional gaggle of dour-faced, bespectacled girls in sweaters and sensible slacks. I felt an odd sisterhood to these women, as if I were witnessing a future version of myself. I sat behind the counter and watched them shuffle from exhibit to exhibit, from the wax Victorian bust showing the effects of corsetry, the organs bunched together in a tight little knot, to the collection of antique IUD's that looked more like distorted paper clips or fishing hooks, and unlike anything anyone would ever want to put inside their body.

I watched them take in the professor's collection of Figerspitzenformers. When the girls learned that women wore these brass "finger shapers," tightening the screws each night to transform their fingertips into "things of beauty," their eyes went wide, their eyebrows disappearing into their bangs.

The professor ended this exhibit with a rousing, impassioned plea to stop the tradition of self-mutilation for the sake of male approval and cultural capital. She talked about the ever-increasing need for feminine empowerment and solidarity. The girls nodded in support, some so emphatically their glasses slipped from their noses. But when the professor commended the girls for not falling prey to pop culture's standards of beauty, for spending their time and energy developing their minds instead of their bodies, it was like a storm cloud passed over the room, and I knew they wouldn't be back.

The next exhibit idea was the albatross skeleton. As we were unpacking that crate, the professor explained how sailors and fishermen in the early 20th century would throw bait hooks in the air and unintentionally snag an albatross. One sailor decided to keep his dead bird for future taxidermy.

"The belief among sailors that killing an albatross is bad luck has been repeatedly referenced," the professor said. "But you know that. You've read Coleridge."

"Sure, of course I have," I said.

I have not.

"Albatrosses mate for life," the professor continued. "That dead bird's mate circled the ship for almost a week. Finally, the crew stormed the sailor's cabin, threatening to throw him overboard unless he surrendered the carcass."

"How did he manage to keep it?"

"A trawler out of the Falklands found him drifting in a lifeboat, dehydrated and delirious, clutching a dead bird. They say it took three men to pry it from his hands."

We hung the skeleton just opposite the entrance to the shop, hoping to utilize its ten-foot wingspan for maximum effect. The professor saw the exhibit as a metaphor for love—the albatross's lifelong commitment to one another, the sailor's devotion to his treasured artifact. We scheduled the debut on Valentine's Day.

Perhaps this should have been obvious from the beginning, but people celebrating that Hallmark holiday of romance don't want to spend their evening looking at the bones of a giant bird. Even the few stragglers that wandered in didn't appreciate the exhibit. They didn't buy it. Not because our fair townspeople didn't believe the story, but because they didn't believe in the existence of albatrosses. More than one patron took in the giant bones, scrunched up their face, and then commented on the mythical nature of the albatross, likening them to, "you know, a dragon or a pterodactyl."

By then the professor had grabbed a bottle of something and retreated to her office. The entire night was a failure, but not for me. I was just happy, for once, to have plans on Valentine's Day.

Even though the you-know-what is due to be delivered any minute, I still have no idea what "it" is. I've asked. Repeatedly. But each time the professor has only offered a vague or meandering response. She's told me what the exhibit will *not* be. She's said it will not be another Malbec-soaked miscalculation. She's said its success won't be dependent upon half-baked assumptions about what people like or want.

"Then what is it?" I said.

"Something that will demand attention and repeat visits."

Now, I watch as the crate is rolled onto the liftgate of the delivery truck and lowered to the ground. On one side are red arrows and letters indicating, This End Up. Others warn, Extremely Heavy. On another side of the crate, stenciled in faded black letters, is Huntsville, Texas. The professor and I roll it inside. Then she hands me one of our pry bars, and we get to work. We each take a side, slowly expanding the seam, slowly inching the nails back through their wooden burrows. The sound is horrible, like we're murdering a goose.

After minutes of pushing and pulling and an ever-increasing burning in my forearms and what I'm sure is at least one splinter in my hand, the side gives way. I peek past the clouds of dust and pine particles to the back of the crate's shadowy hold.

"What the hell is that?" I say.

"That," the professor says with a slight curl to her carmine lips, "is Yellow Mama."

The professor tells me Yellow Mama formerly belonged to the Texas State Penitentiary. During its forty-year run, the chair was used to execute more than three hundred people. Which is disturbing enough, but the chair is also a migraine-inducing, eye-shielding shade of canary yellow.

"What's with that color? Is it supposed to be, like, an additional punishment?"

"The prison contracted some of its inmate labor with the Highway Department," the professor says. "When it came time to paint the chair, the yellow highway line paint was readily available."

The professor gives the chair prime placement in the shop, just beside her collection of World War I facial prosthetics and directly across from Charlotte. She has me spend the next hour dusting and polishing the wood, its merciless luminosity increasing with every swipe. Then I oil the leather helmet and the numerous leather straps that are cracked and discolored from age and sweat and strain. When I'm finished, the chair looks pretty good, considering. But I still don't get it.

"What, exactly, are you struggling to comprehend?" the professor says.

"I mean, sure, the chair is creepy, and it has a dark, disturbing history, and some people will come for that."

"True."

"And I'm sure others will see it as an instrument of justice, a historical bulwark against the rising tide of crime, or whatever."

"Undoubtedly," the professor says.

"But then what? Once the novelty wears off, how do we keep the customers coming back?"

"That's simple," the professor says. "We're going to electrocute them."

As I rumble home in my ratty Corolla, I force the professor's sadistic business scheme from my mind. Home has its own concerns. Just past the pool of brackish water everyone in town refers to as the duck pond—though I've never seen a duck there in my life—is a dead end street. The edge of the state forest consumes one side of the street; the other is populated by a handful of listing houses in various states of dilapidation. The one on the end, with its paint peeling like birch bark and the yard gone feral with neglect—that's mine.

I pull up to find Dad, as always, sitting on the porch in the scant glow of the streetlight. There's a beer bottle in his hand, a Stonehenge of empties at his feet.

"Hiya, honey. How was work?"

"We got a new exhibit."

"That sounds nice."

"Yeah, I'm not so sure."

Dad likes that I work at The Spectacularium. He likes that I have a positive female influence in my life. Ever since we lost my mom, having a positive woman in my life has been kind of a thing for him. I don't have the heart to tell him he's half right.

When I say we "lost" my mom, I don't mean she died. I mean we had her and now we don't, and we don't know where she is. Lost. After spending more than a year watching her own mother succumb slowly to cancer, Mom did an assessment of her life. Apparently, she found it lacking. Not long after the funeral, Mom—discretely, she probably felt—started picking fights with Dad after dinner. Money and Mom's happiness, her potential, were usually the issues, and how the lack of one was stifling, suffocating the others. What began as whispers quickly boiled over into shouts. Mom would go one by one, recounting their marriage's recent failures and historical shortcomings.

"I swear to God, I'm this close to leaving you," she'd eventually say, and from my room, I imagined her hand, the distance between her thumb and index finger. That distance diminishing.

At some point, after enduring this tally of faults, Dad would ask, "Do you even still love me?"

And even though I was unfamiliar with love and relationships, the riddles and ramifications, I knew that if Dad had to ask that question, he already had his answer.

Now Dad spends every night on the porch, sitting in the dark, staring at the woods, waiting for Mom to miraculously emerge from the trees? I don't know.

"Maybe you should think about getting out some," I once said to him in the early days of his nightly vigil.

Dad took a long sip of beer and then made a slow sweep with his hand, gesturing toward the black expanse of the forest, the stars above. "I am out," he said.

I was right. The week we debuted Yellow Mama, people came to see it. To touch it and pose for pictures. To prove to their friends they'd encountered something terrible. We also got the justice-junkies who came to pay their respects to this piece of American history, this reminder that the wages of sin are death. They solemnly marveled at this butter-colored warning of what awaits those who choose Godless lives driven by evil. They, too, took pictures. Then both groups grew bored of the chair and stopped coming. Business slowed, again.

Then this afternoon, when it felt like forever since the bell over the door had dinged, the bell over the door dings. Three guys thunder in, clad in the sweatshirts and track nylon of the community college. They're a whirlwind of kinetic, anticipatory energy. I point them toward the chair, and when they see it, when they read about Yellow Mama's history, the scores of people it's shocked out of existence, their enthusiasm intensifies. They pose for pictures, flexing their muscles and feigning electrified faces. They speak of the chair with a reverential awe, preceding or punctuating their sentences with a booming *Dude!*

"How sick is this, Dude?" says the one in the black sweatshirt.

"Dude, you should totally sit in it," says another in red.

It's during this intellectual exchange when the professor emerges from her office, tall and lean in another black dress, another pair of black heels. She looks like an exclamation point.

"Would you boys like to try the chair?"

"Can we?" one of them says. "Can we sit in it?"

"You can do more than sit in it."

Professor Orbach explains that most modern electric chairs put out 2,000 to 2,200 volts at seven to twelve amps. "I've had this control console rewired to significantly reduce that current. Now we're working with milliamps—or one one-thousandth of the original amount.

It's completely safe," she says. Then she has me hand out legal liability waivers for each guy to sign.

The first one takes a seat, and I help professor use the leather straps to secure his chest, waist, wrist, and ankles to the chair. As she lowers the leather helmet, an expression of unease blooms on his face, and I can't help but think about the first monkey shot into space. The professor raises the leg of his track pants and attaches the brass electrode to his calf. She says they'll start with seven milliamps at five-second intervals.

"You'll feel a slight tingle," she tells him. And then, as she turns to the console, a bit softer, she adds, "And perhaps some involuntary muscular contractions."

The chair is eerily silent. As the current moves through each boy, slightly puppeteering their bodies with its invisible energy, I'm waiting for a whir or a hum. Something. The stuff of movies. But there is nothing. Just silence and the occasional soft knock of the boys' limbs against the wood.

"What did you expect?" the professor says. "You don't hear the electricity in your appliances at home, do you? There isn't a crackling buzz coming from your espresso machine, is there?"

"We don't have an espresso machine."

"Your lamps then."

By the time we finish, the sun is low in the sky, shades of pink and purple yielding to an encroaching darkness. I watch the boys leave. Their eyes look flat, painted-on, but they also smile this spastic collapsing and expanding smile, and bob their heads as if following a rhythm only they can hear.

They come back the next afternoon. And they are different. Their brash energy and hollow bravado are gone, replaced by a meek and respectful manner. Their voices thin and diffident as they ask, "May we use the chair again please?"

"Of course," the professor says. "For a modest fee."

The boys come back again the next day, and they bring their friends.

Now when I arrive at The Spectacularium, it's choked with people. Most pace around the shop, pretending to be interested in the exhibits as their wait for their turn in the chair. Others loiter outside, leaning against the brick, smoking cigarettes.

Now most people know the routine so well the professor has stopped explaining how the chair works. She even allows some customers to make specific output and duration requests, saying, "So, what are we doing today?" as if this is a salon and they are simply getting their hair done. I take their money and have them sign the waiver, and then we shoot them full of silent energy. Afterwards, they stagger from the chair boneless, wobbly as newborn calves. They lean on Charlotte's case until their body solidifies, until they can find their feet and regain their balance.

Now the cases are covered in fingerprints.

After the solitude of my gymnasium lunch, the rubbery yield of the mats and the sour sweat of past submissions, I have Sister Palmer's History of Religion class. Today we're learning about the lives of saints, how many of them engaged in voluntary afflictions to their bodies. We learn about Saint Dominic Loricatus, how he requested hundreds of lashings while reciting the psalms. How Saint Thomas More wore chainmail and coarse hairshirts against his skin. We learn that Saint Francis of Assisi received Christ's stigmata wounds. Sister Palmer tells us these saints underwent these mortifications of the flesh as reminders of their continued sin. She says they believed these forms of self-mutilation would help them grow in virtue and lead to salvation.

I wonder if this explains Yellow Mama's popularity. Its allure. Does the chair help alleviate feelings of guilt? Is the sensation of being shocked, the pain, a kind of bodily penance? I wonder what our customers did to think they deserve it.

Most of the people that come to use Yellow Mama are guys from the community college, strangers to me. But, occasionally, I'll spot someone I know: some of the St. Bart's janitorial staff, Nelson, our mailman. Yesterday, Mr. Venefort came in. He's the owner of Scoops de Ville, a 60's-era auto-themed ice cream parlor, and our town's singular attempt at wit. I used to go there after school, order a hot fudge sundae, and scoot into one of the booths made to resemble a miniature Cadillac. Sometimes Mr. Venefort would give me an extra scoop of vanilla. "Don't tell the boss," he'd say with a wink. But the day he came into the The Spectacularium and saw me behind the counter, he froze at the door. His body tensed, and any resemblance to the affable man muscling out scoops vanished. He turned as if to leave, but then turned back and trudged to the counter. He filled out the waiver and handed over his money. He never once looked at me.

Sister Palmer gives us an in-class writing exercise, then sits at her desk and busies herself with her Bible. Here, too, I am aware of my standing in the St. Bart's social order, and so I sit in the back corner, far from the prancing ponies and their beautiful, lip-glossed wrath. Or maybe not. Because not five minutes into our writing assignment, I look up to see Lexie leading a small cadre of our school's most genetically blessed. They are headed right for me. If Lexie owns an outfit that isn't designed to show off at least three inches of her toned, tan-even-in-December stomach, I've never seen it. Even in December.

Lexie takes a seat at one of the empty desks. "So, you and the witch are, like, electrocuting people now?"

"We're not exactly—"

"I want in."

"What?"

"I want to sit in your weird, yellow chair and have you zap me, or whatever. So, can you do it?"

"Do what?"

"Sneak me in. Duh. You know I can't just go on my own. Not when she's there."

The professor's waiver explicitly states that The Yellow Mama Experience is for adults only. All participants must be at least eighteen years of age.

"Why do you want to use the chair?"

"I know some of the guys from the college."

Of course she does.

"They told me the chair's amazing. Unlike anything they've ever experienced. They said the sensation creates this singular focus, and suddenly there's no more stress, or anxiety, or insecurity."

I wonder what in the holy hell Lexie Curlew of all people has to be insecure about, but she keeps talking.

"They said it's like, when the chair comes on, everything else in your life gets turned off. And that, at some point, you don't even feel the pain anymore, but instead a kind of..."

"Euphoria?"

"I don't speak Spanish."

"Bliss?"

"Yes! It sounds like a trip. So, can you get me in?"

Actually, I can. The shop's been so busy lately Professor Orbach has been leaving early to make the deposits before the bank closes. She had an extra set of keys made so I could lock up. I don't know if it's because I'm disoriented from the glow of Lexie's attention or if there's a part of me that longs to strap her to Yellow Mama and light her up, but I find myself saying, "Yeah. I think so."

Lexie squeezes my arm and emits a high-pitched, glee-filled squeal. "I can't wait."

Sister Palmer looks up from her desk, craning her neck like a turtle. "What's that racket? What are you girls doing back there?"

"Talking about Jesus," Lexie says, flashing a row of perfect, communion wafer-white teeth.

"Good. Good girls."

"Sit with us at lunch tomorrow," Lexie whispers. "We'll figure out the rest."

Later that afternoon, when I pull up to The Spectacularium there are no customers waiting outside. Inside the shop, it is equally empty.

"What happened?" I say to the professor. "Where is everyone?"

"The ice cream guy bought out the hour."

I peer around the corner. Mr. Venefort is slumped in the chair, his chin on his chest, both rising and falling with each ragged breath.

"An hour. Is that even safe?"

"If we limit the output and allow for periods of recovery, then yes. In a manner of speaking. He's currently taking a medically advised timeout."

"Even so. An hour?"

"He is working through some things. From what I understand, he's has been having an affair. I imagine there is some residual guilt."

I look back at Mr. Venefort. He always seemed to have a smile on his face. It was easy to imagine he's had the same short, parted-on-the-side haircut since he was a little boy. Cheating on his wife? "I can't believe it."

"It happens," the professor says.

My face must look expectant, disappointed by her emotional economy, because Professor Orbach then says, "It happened to me."

"Really?"

"We were both teaching then. Martin had just received tenure. We were planning to summer in Borneo to celebrate and search for a particular set of ritualistic funeral masks. A few days before we were scheduled to leave, I learned that Martin had been sneaking around with Melanie, one of his graduate assistants. Then I was informed that she would be replacing me on the trip."

"That's awful."

"Time's up," the professor says, glancing at her watch. "Come. Help me with the ice cream man."

I tighten the leather straps around Mr. Venefort. I lower the helmet. He still doesn't look at me.

Professor Orbach dials up twelve milliamps and then flips the switch. "Melanie was a gumdrop of a girl," she says. "She had no business traipsing around the risk and rot of the jungle. Naturally, she gets hurt. She cuts her hand pretty seriously, and it gets infected and gangrene sets in. Some shaman/medicine man had to lop it off before poor Melanie lost her entire arm."

"What happened?"

"Martin still got his funeral masks, which were all he really cared about. His precious artifacts were all he ever cared about."

"I meant to Melanie."

"Yes. Of course. Martin saw her back to America but they parted ways soon afterwards. He was an aesthetic at heart and could never abide a one-handed lover. Most men, I've found, are so obsessed with the physical, whereas we women are more character driven. Content oriented. I've often thought how my love life would have been far less complicated had I been a lesbian. What's your preference, dear?"

"I like guys, I think."

"Shame." Professor Orbach kills the power to the chair though

Mr. Venefort's body continues rattling for a few seconds. Eventually it stills, then deflates a little. "It didn't help matters that that shaman did something of a shoddy job, though one can hardly blame him. Martin later said—"

"You continued to speak to him?"

"We continued to do more than speak."

"But he lied to you. He betrayed you."

"Oh dear, you're young still. You'll come to find that age has a way of modifying emotions, of offering a context. Martin and I were still married, were still early in our careers and trying to build our collection. He always had a bit of hound in him. I knew that. All exciting men do, or at least those who perceive themselves as exciting. Plus, it's not as if I wasn't without my dalliances. Desire is not gender specific." Then she leans in front of Mr. Venefort. "A bit more?" she says, and he nods his head, grunts out a beleaguered, "Yes."

The professor increases the output to fifteen milliamps, juices him again. "Where were we?"

"Melanie. Her hand."

"Yes. I was telling you about that shaman's handiwork, such as it was. Martin said Melanie's stump had bits of dying, discolored flesh dangling from it, like it was wrapped in bad prosciutto." Again, she shuts off the chair.

I tilt my head toward Mr. Venefort, who has a silvery stream of drool leaking from his lips. "Is that normal?"

"Oh. It's unappealing, but not surprising. Temporary paralysis of some minor muscles can occur beyond a certain output. Perhaps we should start renting bibs." Then she hits him with another jolt.

"Did you ever see Melanie again?"

"I tried to be cordial, establish a conciliatory correspondence. I, too, was once a young woman who fell prey to Martin's charm. Though, admittedly, I fared a bit better than poor Melanie," Professor Orbach says, grinning and wiggling her fingers at me. "Still, I reached out. I discovered Melanie's birthday and sent her a gorgeous set of juggling clubs from the early days of the Moscow circus. I never received a thank you card."

By the time we finish Mr. Venefort's session, his face is clenched and glazed in sweat. He's grinding his teeth, but from the sound of it, he may as well be chewing rocks. He won't—can't—let go of the chair's armrests, and I have to peel his fingers free one by one. I expect him to feel hot, toasted, but his skin is clammy to the touch. Mr. Venefort's too incapacitated to drive, so the professor calls him a cab. When it arrives, we gather him up and pour him inside.

When we're back inside, I see that Mr. Venefort has left behind a sweat shadow on the chair, a glistening imprint that magnifies the paint's penetrating gloss.

I wonder if I'm expected to clean that.

I wonder what the hell just happened.

"Are we lobotomizing people?" I say.

"Technically speaking, a lobotomy is a surgical procedure, so—"

"I'm serious. What are we doing? Has this been your plan all along?"

"Try to understand, people have problems."

"Not everyone," I say, eager to argue.

"Yes. Everyone. Especially the ones that think they don't."

This sounds more right than I want to admit.

"People have problems," the professor continues, "and sometimes they need a reprieve, something to quiet their minds and offer a temporary escape from those problems. We, the chair, are providing that."

"Mr. Venefort didn't seem like he's escaping his problems. Or if he is, if he's forgetting them, it's because we're melting his mind."

Professor Orbach sighs and leans against the wall beside Charlotte's case. I look from one to the other, and their expressions—the cold eyes, the aggravated frowns—look eerily similar.

"Do you have any idea how difficult this business is?" the professor says. "How hard it is to acquire these artifacts? It's one big boy's club. At every turn, I'm competing with some fool in a safari shirt who fancies himself the next Indiana Jones." The professor gestures around her. "This is a lifetime of work, of struggle and sacrifice, and no one cared. No one in this town cared about any of this until I got that chair."

She's right, I know that; but it doesn't change how I feel, and I say as much. "It doesn't seem like we're helping people. It seems like we're hurting them."

"No one is forcing these people to use the chair," she says. "Just like no one is forcing you to work here." Then Professor Orbach disappears into the dark of her office, returning moments later with her purse. She points to Yellow Mama on her way out the door. "Be sure to clean that up before you leave."

This need to assert myself, to condemn the professor's actions and not be seen as her ally, stays with me right up until I meet Lexie. As promised, we talked at lunch, and I hate to admit it, but being there in the cafeteria, sitting with her and the rest of the prancing ponies and knowing everyone else in the cafeteria could see me sitting there, was intoxicating. And, even if after Lexie and I settled on a time to meet outside of the shop, she and the ponies promptly left me alone at the table, so what? I'm not dwelling on it. I was still in the cafeteria, still eating my lunch among other people, if not necessarily with them, and that felt like progress.

That night, I find that Dad's left his porch post long enough to make some dinner. Ever since Mom left, dinner has been mostly frozen pizzas, and, occasionally, one of those salads in a bag because Dad feels guilty about all of the pizza.

Dad is staring. I can feel his eyes on me as I push the salad around my plate, pick out the pieces of wilted lettuce.

"What?" I say.

"What? Nothing. I just...how are you?"

"Fine."

"I heard some interesting things about your work, about this chair you two have. What's the story with that?"

"Oh, you know," I say. But he doesn't and I refuse to elaborate. We eat our slices in silence.

"I miss your mother," Dad eventually says. Mumbles.

I tell him that Mom misses him too and that she just needs some time and will likely be back soon. Neither of us believes me, my lies as apparent as the pizza between us, but it doesn't matter. Actually, I'm grateful for these moments. I'm so busy helping Dad deal with the fact that Mom left him I don't have time to think about how she left me too.

Dad nibbles at the end of a slice, then gives up, pushes the plate away. He stands, grabs a beer from the fridge and heads for the porch. When I leave to meet Lexie a couple of hours later, he's still out there.

"Where're you headed?" he says, his gaze fixed on the trees.

"I'm meeting a friend."

Dad turns to me, and the look on his face, the competing mixture of surprise and joy because he knows what a rare occasion this is, breaks my heart. I'm down the steps and halfway in my car when he yells from the porch.

"I'm trying, you know?"

Dad used to say the same thing to Mom during one of her tirades. It usually made them worse.

"Okay."

I meet Lexie by the back door of The Spectacularium. She wanders around the shop while I warm up the console.

"Oh my God," she says in response to just about every exhibit. "This place is like a nightmare factory. How do you work here?"

More and more, I've been wondering that myself.

"Check it out," Lexie says. "It's, what, some kind of hair crown? Am I Queen of the Hair People?"

I turn and see Lexie has placed one of the professor's memento moris on her head, this one a small wreath made from the hair of, I believe, three generations of deceased women. But I don't tell Lexie that. Her shrill reaction would alert half the town.

"Yes, it's a crown. You're a queen," I tell her, and Lexie beams.

Yellow Mama's maximum output is fifty milliamps, "far from fatal," according to Professor Orbach, though lately I have my doubts. After I secure Lexie to the chair, ignoring the squeal she emits when the waist strap touches her exposed stomach, a delicious fantasy develops in my mind. I could crank the chair all the way up, giving Lexie a single, soul-shattering jolt, an overdue retribution for a history of fat jokes.

But I don't do that either. Instead I dial up an introductory eight milliamps and send Lexie's body buckling with electric abandon.

"That was awesome," she says afterwards, still basking in her bliss spasm. Lexie has sweat-slick strands of hair plastered to her face, and this ridiculous, slack-jawed smile, but she still, somehow, looks gorgeous. She tries to stand and stumbles into my arms, and even though I know the chair is off, I swear, when her body touches mine, I feel a little charge.

We meet again the next night. On the third night, Lexie says we have to meet later than usual, something about her parents, a dinner party. I think about heading home, having another pizza with Dad.

But then I wonder just how late he'd let me leave to meet Lexie. Not that I think he'd do something so uncharacteristically parental as citing a curfew, but still. Instead I get some fast food, sit in the parking lot picking my way through a burger and bag of fries. I try calling home, but of course, Dad doesn't pick up.

Lexie is already waiting by the back door when I arrive. When I open it I see some of the lights are on. I can hear the professor's voice and then another. A man's voice. Quieter, muffled, but definitely deeper.

"Wait here," I tell Lexie.

As I walk into the shop, I think about poor Mr. Venefort undergoing another session. I wonder how much more punishment he believes he deserves, and if his body, his mind, will survive the process.

But when I enter the main room, it's not Mr. Venefort in the chair, not his body spasming against the straps, not his eyes rolled back into his head, the whites turned a sour yellow. It's my dad.

I don't know what the professor has the chair set to, but whatever it is, it's too much.

"Stop! Stop it," I say, running to the console and killing power to the chair. "What are you doing?" I say to Dad, and then again, but much louder, to Professor Orbach. My head swivels desperately from one to the other. Neither answers. My face gets hot, and my vision swims. I tilt my head back, willing away the tears.

"I was under the impression that you knew," the professor says.

"Well, I didn't."

"That's unfortunate," the professor says. "Secrets can be damaging." Then her gaze moves over my shoulder, just past me.

I turn around, and there's Lexie.

"I know you're using the chair to...make friends," the professor says.

Lexie and I look at one another. Her eyebrows knit together as her lips curl with disgust.

"No," I say. "I'm not."

Dad coughs out something wet and reverberating. He squirms around in the chair, trying to free himself from the straps. I move to help him, kneeling down to remove the electrode and release his feet.

"Why didn't you tell me?" I whisper.

Dad's hair hangs in his eyes. Sweat drips from his nose. When he looks up at me, it's like he's aged a dozen years, the lines on his face cut deeper and darker.

"My first time," he says between labored breaths. "I wanted to see if it could help me feel different. Better."

I know the question I have to ask next, and I'm going to, but not right now. Not just this second. Because Dad's answer—whether the chair did or didn't—is going to change everything, complicate everything, and I'm not sure I'm ready for that.

There's the tick of heels on the hardwood. I feel two hands wrap around my arms, the metallic chill of many rings. They muscle me to my feet.

"Perhaps you should have a seat," the professor says.

Camp Vampire Kids

Mom and I are driving to camp and playing the game where we think of jobs I could one day have that won't *compromise my condition*. That's how she phrases it. Mom and I spend a lot of time avoiding things that might compromise my condition.

"What about a blackjack dealer in Vegas?" I say.

Mom groans in that way that makes her nostrils flare.

"What's wrong with that? There are no windows, plus casinos are busier at night."

"So are emergency rooms. You could be a doctor."

"You always say that," I say, then turn and stare out the window. We pass a field and some white cows that look purple through the protective tint. "I could be a bouncer."

"Yeah?"

"At a strip club."

Mom takes her eyes off of the road just long enough to look me over—all elbows and knees and reedy angles. "Who are *you* going to bounce?"

"Hey!"

She smiles and blows me a kiss.

The game continues. Mom and I go back and forth, suggesting jobs that are noble and practical (hers) or silly and adventurous (mine).

What we don't say, what we never talk about, is that I'll be lucky if I live long enough to do any of them.

Mom pulls the car onto an off-ramp. "We need gas. You coming inside?"

I nod.

"Then get your gear on."

"I don't need it. I'll just run from the car to the store. I won't get burned."

Mom hits me with the full wattage of her pleading gaze. "Can we please not do this? Not again?"

"Fine."

Mom and I also stopped at a gas station the first year we went to camp. We were lost and went inside for directions. I had my gear on then too—the gloves, the jumpsuit, the face shield. I remember the man behind the counter, the way he stared at me even when Mom started speaking to him.

"Craryville?" he finally said, dragging his eyes from me to Mom. "What do you want to go there for?"

"We're headed to Camp Fun Without the Sun," Mom said, and when the man asked what that was, she told him about the camp and the kinds of kids that go there.

"Yeah?" he said, a smirk stretching across his face. "Like little monsters? Little vampires?" He turned to me, brought his fists to his mouth, and made fangs with his index fingers. Then he hissed.

Mom lost her mind. Truly. There was a moment of micro-insanity where she just screamed questions at the cashier—*What the hell is your problem? What kind of person are you? Can't you see he's just a little boy?*—things like that.

The man didn't know any of the answers.

Mom put a hand on my shoulder, steered me towards the door. Then she stopped, turned around, and kicked over a display of Cool Ranch Doritos.

She was still fuming as we bounced along the camp's gravel driveway and entered the clearing in the Craryville forest. The other mothers took us inside, sat Mom down, poured her a jelly jar of white wine. They told her how they'd all been there before, how they'd all heard some version of judgment and cruelty spit at their kids. How people follow them through stores, snapping not-so-surreptitious pictures with their phones.

"Some jackass asks if my son is a vampire at least once a week," one of the mothers confessed. "Which is just so stupid. So ridiculous."

And it is. When I met Cameron a little later, he was, with his chubby cheeks and ginger crew cut, the least vampire-looking kid I have ever seen.

We've also been called Midnight's Children, Children of the Moon, Children of the Night, Shadow Kids, Nightwalkers, and Night Dwellers. Other people simply point or stare, exchanging whispers and laughter in a classless language all its own. But the most common attempt at creativity, the pejorative we hear again and again, is Vampire Kids.

I wish it were accurate. Imagine a vampire. Now take away the strength and the speed and the immortality, and what are you left with? A pale guy with a terminal reaction to the sun. That's who I am.

That's who we all are.

We're all born this way, but our genetic disorder lays dormant for a while. Depending on the particular variant, we'll get anywhere from four to six years of day living before it kicks on. Four to six years of pool parties and playgrounds. Of normalcy. Of friends.

I was lucky. I was eight when my immune system could no longer protect my body from the sun. Cameron jokes I was a late wilter.

Then, I was young enough that Mom could coax me into my gear by playing to my imagination and sense of make-believe. She'd remind me that my UV-protectant jumpsuit was the kind astronauts wore. She called it my "special costume," and, for a while, it did make me feel special. Unique. Now it makes me feel like a freak everywhere I go. Everywhere but here.

Mom and I are one of the last families to arrive. We park beside the camp's main building: a long, single-story structure with dorm rooms on each side, and a kitchen and dining hall in the center. Us kids bunk up on one side of the building so we can stay up all night, watch movies, and play video games. The moms stay on the other side so they can talk, and drink wine, and sometimes cry and hug each other when they think we're not watching.

It's always pretty dark in here. Shadowy patches are intermittently interrupted by the faint glow of a few Edison bulbs. The building has plenty of windows, which are covered with a UV-protectant film, but they're also draped in a coal-black fabric with the heft and thickness of Victorian theater curtains. Dan and Karen don't like to take any chances. Mom and I have the same tint on our windows back home, but she, too, takes the curtain precaution. Our house doesn't get a lot of light either. All of our plants are plastic.

I shed my gear, and when my eyes adjust, I race down the hallway to my room and find Cameron. He's sitting cross-legged on his bunk amid piles of clothes and DVDs and video games. Cameron and I have been roommates at camp for the past four years, and since then, his method of "unpacking" has been to just dump everything on his bed, retrieving items as needed.

"Check it out," he says, holding up his copy of *Time Fighters II*. "You will soon succumb to the awesome power of my Mayan warrior."

"Yeah? Not if my knight's broadsword has anything to say about it."

"You two are a couple of dorks."

I look over and see Hannah lying on my bunk, her black hair fanned out on my white pillowcase like inverted starlight.

I met Hannah last year, her first at camp. A bunch of us were in the game room, flopped on beanbags, watching a movie. She came in and sat on the small square of available carpet beside me. I noticed the faint band of cinnamon-colored dots that run under each of Hannah's eye and over the bridge of her nose. "I like your freckles," I said, which, admittedly, is not the smoothest line ever uttered in the history of mankind (it's probably not even the smoothest line in the history of that game room), but even so, Hannah smiled, brought a self-conscious hand to her face.

"Thanks," she said. "The result of my moonbathing I guess."

I know she was joking, but I still couldn't help myself from picturing Hannah in her backyard, in a bikini, supine in a band of silver light. I almost fell off my beanbag.

And now here she is again. After the grim limbo of home-schooled loneliness, she's back in *my* room, on *my* bunk, grinning that she's caught me in a moment of unguarded nerdery. It's fine. Hannah can criticize our video game obsession all she wants, but we all know that she's logged more hours in the *Time Fighters* arena than Cam and I put together.

When the rest of the kids and moms have settled in, Dan and Karen gather everyone in the dining hall.

"Helloooo campers," Dan resounds with his usual showman flare, smiling through his beard that's gone grayer since last summer.

The lighting from the Edison bulbs lends a theatrical glow to the dining room. It's an effect Dan embraces. It's a behavior Karen tolerates.

"Karen and I are happy to see a lot of familiar faces and to welcome some new families."

I look around and spot some new kids, maybe five or six years old, most likely recently diagnosed. I envy them. They sit beside their mothers, giddy at the prospect of a week filled with games and playmates, and no such thing as a bedtime. They don't yet know how camp also offers a break from the outright judgment or veiled pity of strangers. They haven't yet come to depend on it.

Dan continues his speech. He runs through the schedule of field trips and nocturnal activities, the ways in which all of us will spend the week "embracing the night." Then Dan introduces Katie, his and Karen's daughter, and the reason they started this camp.

Katie is the oldest person with our condition. Not just here at camp, or in the country, but in the world. When I first came here, I didn't think much about that, or maybe I thought it was cool. But now I sometimes lie awake and think about how difficult and lonely that fact must be. Katie is the living embodiment of all of our hopes and, at the same time, all of our fears.

She'll be twenty-five in August.

Katie is in charge of the junior counselors, and now that we're thirteen, Cameron, Hannah and I are old enough to qualify. She welcomes each of us back, reminds us of our various duties and responsibilities. She tells us the Assignment Board will be finished after dinner. Then, while the rest of the campers finish unpacking, the moms head to the kitchen to prepare a feast.

It's mainly moms that accompany us kids to camp. Some of the dads who live close enough and can get away for the weekend drive up for the last two days. Those days are always hard for Mom.

Dad didn't take my diagnosis well. He always enjoyed a beer or two after work, but the day we came back from the doctor's, I watched him pull a bottle of bourbon from the top of the fridge and drink from it straight. He started going out more and more, staying out later and later. One night, he climbed into the back of a police car and demanded to be taken to an establishment called "The Tit Mouse." When the officer informed Dad that was he not a cab driver, and his cruiser was not a taxi, Dad became what would later be described as "insolent."

So, some Thursday night/Friday morning, this cop knocked on our door only to find the sleep-smeared face of an eight-year-old on the other side. Mom was working nights then.

"You here all alone?" he said.

"My dad is supposed to be watching me."

The cop spent the next few seconds looking at me, and then over at his cruiser where Dad was slumped against the window, asleep in the backseat. The cop had this look on his face, as if the effort of turning from me to his car was causing him a deep and mysterious pain. Eventually, he let Dad go, saying that he wasn't going to arrest him because Dad had no priors. Which I didn't understand. At the time, I thought "priors" was police slang for priorities. It turns out that cop and I were both right.

Mom tried to defend Dad, telling me that he was just scared and confused. She said that, given time, he would be back to his old self. But less than a year after that night, Dad left us and moved to Phoenix, a place that averages 351 days of sunshine a year. So enough about Dad.

As I'm finishing my second helping of Karen's lasagna, I see that Katie has somehow intuited my most secret of desires, or it's just a stroke of amazing fortune, but either way, I'm overjoyed when I check the Assignment Board. Hannah and I have been assigned Lifeguard Duty for Midnight Swim.

Dan and Karen buy glow-in-the-dark items in bulk. I sit on the dock, watching a lake teeming with phosphorescent beach balls, Frisbees, and pool noodles. Neon green inner tubes glowing like giant radioactive doughnuts. Campers splash around, and luminescent blues and greens and yellows reflect and ripple in the dark water, the colors pulsing and undulating like some submerged aurora borealis. Hannah sits beside me, our legs dangling off the edge of the dock, our feet in the water. Our knees nowhere close to touching.

I think about mentioning my aurora borealis comparison to Hannah. Things haven't been going as well as I'd hoped. I've spent the majority of our shift trying not to stare at Hannah, then smiling awkwardly and quickly looking away when she catches me. Instead, I tell her about the *Ipomoea Alba,* how it's a night-blooming morning glory. I don't tell Hannah I know this because it was the topic of my botany paper. Mrs. Sedota, my online science teacher, let me choose it. When I admitted I selected that flower because I thought Hannah would like it, that it would give us something to talk about, Mrs. Sedota said I had "admirable foresight."

But now as I hear the words spill from my head, I realize that only someone who doesn't really interact with other people would think their science paper a suitable source of flirty banter.

"It's commonly called the moonflower," I say, "because when its alabaster petals unfold, they resemble a full moon."

"That's...cool," Hannah says. Then she raises her eyebrows, offers a slack-tightrope smile.

Even in the dark, I can tell it's a look of forced interest. I wish one of the campers would start drowning and save me.

"Yeah," I continue, like an idiot. "Even though many people consider the moonflower beautiful during the day, it's at night when they really come alive. Kind of like—"

You. *Like* you. Like *you*. Just say it. Why can't I say it?

"Kind of like—"

"Mushrooms," Cameron yells as he rumbles past us, leaps from the end of the dock, and cannonballs into the lake.

Later that night, Cam and I are in the game room, slumped on beanbags, awash in the kaleidoscopic glow of *Time Fighters II*. The *Time Fighters* franchise allows players to choose warriors from various epochs and then battle to the death. Mom doesn't care for the violence, but it's not like she can tell me to go outside and play either. Currently, my medieval knight is getting his gallant ass handed to him by Cameron's Mayan warrior.

"You should just tell her how you feel," he says. "Let her know how infatuated you are."

"Who?"

Cam is good enough at *Time Fighters* to turn away from the screen, to stare at me and through my bullshit while still fending off attacks from my knight. If there is a perk to a life spent indoors and with little social interaction, it is that we are all excellent at video games.

"Yeah, fine, I like Hannah. But I wouldn't say I'm infatuated with her."

"You spent all of last summer writing her that poem. Comparing her skin to...what was it...midnight snow?"

It was moonlit snow, and I only spent half the summer working on it. Not like it matters. Not like I gave Hannah the poem, or even finished writing it.

Cameron nails my knight twice with his Jaguar Claw Strike before I can parry with my broadsword.

"Either way, you better get moving," he says. "Her mom told my mom they might not being coming back next year."

"What? Like not coming back to camp? Why not?"

Cameron shrugs his shoulders. Then his character catches mine upside the head with his obsidian war club. There are cartoonish bursts of bright red gore, and I'm a goner.

The next afternoon, I roll over from a nap to find Hannah standing over my bed. She's backlit by this soft, ethereal white light. She looks like an angel, and I must be dreaming.

"You have a lot of drool on your pillow," she says. "Like, more than seems normal."

"What?" I sit up. "What's happening?"

"Check it out," Hannah says, and then steps aside to reveal the window, its curtains drawn, and beyond them a sky choked with clouds the color of dirty cotton.

I can't decide which is more beautiful—the view from the window or the smile on Hannah's face. These shadowless gray days have, over the years, come to represent one indelible thing: freedom. The freedom to be outside during the day, to feel, however briefly, like ordinary kids. By the time we scramble to the door, Mom is already there, measuring the UV index with her solar meter. It's a 0.8, the lower end of the potential threat spectrum. Still, Mom groans.

"I'll wear a hat."

"And long sleeves," she says.

"Fine."

I change clothes, and Mom warns me not to smile at the sky so my braces don't get struck by lightning. Then she laughs. Because yes, as if having an extremely rare and deadly allergy to the sun wasn't enough of a genetic kick in the dick, I also have crooked teeth.

I return to the clearing just as Cameron and Katie have almost finished picking teams for kickball. Cameron has snagged Hannah. It's between me and Jacob, one of the new five-year-olds, who is running around chasing a grasshopper. It's Katie's pick. We lock eyes. I try to project a neutrality, to suppress all emotion, but my face must not be cooperating because Katie shoots me a sly, knowing grin. Then she picks Jacob.

Cameron places Hannah in center field because she possesses an athletic grace, a seemingly effortless speed. Cameron sticks me in far leftfield because I do not. Just as we're about to run to our positions, Hannah removes her hoodie. She's wearing a white tank top underneath. Even with the cloud cover, this is a careless and dangerous degree of exposure. I think about saying something. Then I notice how Hannah's tank top allows some of her black bra strap to wink through, and I keep my mouth shut.

Instead, I think about what Cam said.

"Dan told me they might put in a zip line next year," I shout across the outfield. "That'll be pretty cool, huh?"

"Yeah. Maybe," she shouts back.

"Maybe. Why maybe?"

Hannah points toward home. Mom is up. She does a little shimmy at the plate, rubs her toes in the dirt like a bull about to charge. Then she smiles and waves to me.

"Move back," Hannah says. "She's got a good leg."

"What? No she doesn't."

But Hannah shakes her palm at me, urging me farther back, farther away. I walk towards her.

"Hey. You're coming back next year, right?"

"Maybe. My mom is still deciding."

"Deciding what?"

And then, sure enough, a deep, rubbery *whomp* rings out across the field, and Mom sends one flying into the gray sky.

Hannah sprints across the field, gets underneath the ball just in time to pluck it from the air. She throws the ball back to the pitcher but doesn't jog back to her position.

"Deciding what?" I shout once more. And then again.

But Hannah just stands there, staring at home plate, not answering.

Just as we get our third out, the clouds begin to dissipate, and the sky shifts from gray to blue like battlefield smoke, and we all run for cover.

Hannah's been assigned Dish Duty for dinner, and I don't see her again until we're all headed to the fire pit. Dan builds a bonfire, and we sit around it, listening to the crickets and cicadas, staring at light-drunk moths that fly too close to the flames. We listen to Dan's scary stories about the spectral inhabitants of nearby farmhouses or the variety of monsters that lurk in the woods. His stories are silly, or dramatic, but overall ineffective at inducing fright. None of us kids are afraid of the dark. As someone starts strumming a guitar for a sing-along, I see Hannah stand up. She walks halfway around the fire pit, nudges my foot with hers.

"Wanna go for a walk?"

We head into the forest. A summer breeze swirls through the branches, the leaves, making their moon shadows flutter. We arrive at the lake, shed our shoes, and walk around its bank. I feel the cool hug of mud around my feet.

"Sorry about this afternoon," Hannah says.

"S'okay."

"It's just that my mom didn't want me to say anything until we knew for sure."

"That you're not coming back?"

"That I'm getting better."

"What?"

We stop walking. Hannah stares at the moonlit lake, its inky shimmer. Then her face breaks into a huge smile. "It's actually kind of amazing."

Hannah tells me how her dermatologist has been incrementally increasing her exposure to UV light, and that, so far, she hasn't been burned.

"I don't know what to say," I tell her, because I don't.

"I know, right? I think my doctor is even more excited than my parents. He says I'm like one in a million. Can you believe that?"

Yes.

"We're still being careful, making sure I respond well to the treatments and that my tolerance is increasing, but if it's true, just think about it."

I do. I imagine Hannah outside during the day, walking along a beach, playing in a park. I imagine her with other kids, and while their faces are blurry, nondescript, I clearly see them basking in the sun's warm glow. They are unharmed and unafraid. They are not me.

I feel my face flush, and my vision goes watery with tears. I wipe my eyes before Hannah notices, grateful, once again, for the dark.

"So you're not coming back to camp then?"

"Well, I mean, not if I'm getting better. Mom thinks we should give the spot to someone more—"

"Sick?"

"Deserving." Hannah cocks her head and what's left of her smile falls. "Are you mad at me?"

We just stand there for a second. Fireflies blink on and off. Sounds from the sing-along drift through the silence. *This Little Light of Mine.* I never minded that song, if I even thought about it at all, but now the lyrics sound sickeningly sweet.

"No. You would be missed is all. Cameron and I would miss you."

"Aww," Hannah says, leaning in for a hug. "I'd miss you guys, too.

You two are like my best buds here."

And while I'm so grateful to be this close to Hannah, to feel her body against mine, to have her arms wrapped around me, I'm even more grateful that she can't see my face.

Later that night, we all load up into a rented school bus. Dan stands at the front, tells us we're getting a special midnight tour of the Albany Zoo. Whoops and cheers bounce around me, echoing throughout the bus's metal interior. We wander through the Reptile House, staring at snakes and lizards indifferent to our curiosity. We see zebras asleep in the middle of a field, huddled together in a herd of black and white. The grand finale of our tour is the tiger exhibit. A crescent moon of moms and campers belly-up to the enclosure's concrete railing. Soon there's the clang of an unseen gate, and a group of tigers slowly pad out into the night. Everyone is instantly captivated—by the deep orange of their fur, their stripes as black as a new moon night. By the two cubs who drink from a makeshift watering hole, the pink wink of their tongues. Even Cameron nudges me in the side with his elbow, points to a massive tiger raking his claws along the length of a log.

A zookeeper tells us that most of these tigers were born here, which means in captivity. Which means they are forced to ignore their nocturnal instincts, to conform to the zoo's daytime schedule and perform for its sunlit pageantry.

That's what I see anyway. I see a group of animals who look angry and annoyed at being awakened to entertain some sick kids. I see their orange fur turned a sickly yellow in the light of the zoo's sodium arc lamps. I see one tiger rub its head along the side of another, both of them making a low, repetitive, guttural sound. The zookeeper tells us this is called "chuffing," that it's the way tigers greet one another.

Tiger chuffing sounds like Mom blowing her nose when she has a cold.

Over in the far corner of the enclosure, I spot a medium-sized tiger. She stares right at me, narrowing her eyes and flashing her fangs. Then she turns her back to me, lifts her tail, and shoots out a jet of pee.

On the bus ride back to camp, I take one of the seats in the back, sprawl out and feign sleep so no one can sit next to me, so no one will bother me. It works for a while. (I use the bus's occasional bumps to sneak a peek.) We hit what feels like a pretty good pothole, and I peek Hannah's legs beside my seat. She must know that I'm faking, that I'm not really asleep, because she stands there for a really long time. I force my eyes all the way shut, and when I crack them open again, she's gone.

At some point, my sleep feigning must work because I doze off. The next thing I know, Mom is shaking me awake. We're back at camp, back just before sunrise, the sky purpling, a red thread of light on the horizon. Everyone scurries inside and gets ready for bed.

Maybe it's because I napped on the bus, but I have trouble falling asleep. I spend a few hours tossing and turning or staring at the ceiling. Finally, I sit up. I pull the curtains aside. Sunlight streams in through the tint, lending a lavender glow to the room.

Why does Hannah get to be better? What makes her so special? I think, even though I could answer that question a hundred different ways.

But maybe it's not just Hannah. Maybe the rest of us can get better too, can start being normal again. Maybe we already are.

I get up and dig through the dresser for some clothes. Cameron rustles in his sleep, cocooned among his treasures like some Egyptian Pharaoh. As I ease the door closed and make my way through the hallway's shadowy emptiness, I think about my odds, the way hope can quickly devolve into delusion. I know I'm not getting better, and I hate that Hannah is. I want her to be sick and weird, like me. With me. I'd rather Hannah be sick and with me than healthy and with someone else.

Maybe that cashier all those years ago was right. Maybe I am monster.

I grab the handle of the front door and take a breath.

Maybe if this doesn't work out, I deserve what I get.

Some kids have said getting burned feels like being stung by a cloud of bees; others imagine it's like getting pierced with hundreds of arrows—an invisible assault that is both localized and all-encompassing. But when I step outside and into the clearing, all I feel is the sun's warmth on my skin. It's a sensation that, after years of dormancy, ignites so many memories. Picnics in the park. Fourth of July parades. Dad and I at the beach, playing in the waves, and then secreting some seawater back to the sand to pour on Mom's back.

But then something happens. The warmth grows hotter and hotter, almost as if someone is turning a dial, exponentially increasing the output of sunlight. My memories get eclipsed by a searing pain, the sun's needle teeth tearing into my arms and face. I have trouble catching my breath. It feels like I'm drowning in heat. I try heading back towards the safety of the building, but doing so makes me dizzy. Pockets of nausea bloom and burst in my throat. My vision goes blurry. The cars in the parking lot and the woods beyond melt into one another.

The sky swirls, or I do, but either way, I stumble and find myself on my hands and knees. The waxy blades of grass feel cool to the touch, and there is a blink of relief as my face is out of the sun, shielded by the back of my head. The pull to stay like this, to somehow crawl inside the safety my own shadow, is too strong, and my body goes limp.

I wake up in my room. A dull but persistent heat pulses from my body. I can feel my heart beat behind my eyes. Mom sits on the edge of my bed, applying aloe to my arm, which is swollen and blistered and the raw, inflamed color of a glazed ham. Mom must feel my eyes on her because she stops, lifts her head. Her face is puffy and slick with tears. Her eyes are as red as my arms.

"Hi," I say.

"What the hell? What were you thinking?"

"I'm sorry."

"No," she yells, startling us both. Two new tears leak from her eyes and trail down her face. "That's not good enough. You have to give me more than that."

So I tell her about Hannah. About how she's getting better, and how envious and angry and scared that makes me.

"I don't understand," Mom says. "Aren't you happy for her?"

"Yes. And no. Not completely. If Hannah gets better, she'll start a different life. She'll no longer need us. She'll leave and she won't come back."

"What makes you think she'd do that?"

"Dad did."

Mom goes silent. The wrinkle between her eyes deepens, and her mouth moves as if to say something, but nothing comes out.

I place my hand on her balled fist, give it a squeeze. "How long was I out there?"

"Two minutes. Maybe less. Katie saw you go outside."

"Is she the one that—?"

"Yes."

"Oh shit," I say, and Mom's eyes widen. "Sorry. Is she okay?"

"She got some minor burns. She says you're heavier than you look."

We just sit together for a while. Then Mom finishes applying the aloe and bandages my arms. She gives me some aspirin, tells me to get some rest.

The throaty rumble of the bus's engine wakes me up. Dan and Karen are taking everyone to Mega-Fun Zone, a bowling alley/arcade that touts the largest Laser Tag arena in upstate New York.

When they're gone, I decide I need some air. I get up and get dressed, wincing with each movement. I shuffle down to the fire pit, ease myself down in one of the Adirondack chairs. A breeze blows in from the clearing, cooling my skin and stinging it at the same time. Birds—or if you believe Dan's stories, bats—flit through the trees.

I hear the rustle of leaves and swing my flashlight to the source, illuminating Katie's face. She shields her eyes, and I kill the beam.

"You didn't want to go bowling?"

"Nah," she says. "The used shoes gross me out."

"Thanks for saving me. I'm sorry you got hurt."

"No big thing." Katie waves off my apology, but I can see her hand is bandaged. She sits beside me.

"Still. Thank you."

"Of course. You know this morning was the first time in almost nineteen years that I've felt the sun on my skin. With each birthday the doctors and reporters return, marveling at another year, another record set. They all want to know what I'm doing, how I'm outwitting our disease. But in all of these years, none of them ever bothered to ask if I'm happy."

"And are you?"

"I am today. I felt needed. Instead of just hiding in the shadows, waiting for the sun to set, I got to save you from doing something stupid."

I pick up a twig, toss it into the pile of ashes and charred logs. "I wasn't trying to hurt myself. I just—"

"Wanted to feel normal? To feel like an ordinary kid and not a freak?"

"Yes. Exactly."

"I get it. You liked someone who didn't necessarily feel the same way?"

"Yeah."

"And in the anger and confusion of your heartache you did something foolish?"

"I suppose so."

Katie stands and smiles. She pats me on the shoulder with her burned hand. "Well then, you're in luck. Because that's about as normal as it gets."

Boat Guy

I like to romanticize adventures. These are usually grand, revelatory experiences, from which I emerge a new and better person. One of them involves a cabin deep in the woods. In it, I channel my inner Thoreau, and free from the trappings of television, and phones, and the Internet, I can finally suspend my decades-long practice of gross procrastination and write the book that will confirm my gifts and genius to the rest of humanity. I haven't tried that one yet, but I plan to get around to it.

Another one finds me on a sailboat. Here, I picture myself out in the middle of the Pacific. Each day begins with a majestic, God-affirming sunrise, which can only be outdone by the tranquil beauty of its sunset counterpart. My days are filled with the challenge of capturing and honing the wind as I make my way through the great expanse of water and sky, intoxicated by so much blue.

One night there is a terrible storm. Mother Nature releases her awful fury, and I am on the deck of the boat, fighting to steady the ship. Fighting to stay alive. Waves crash against the bow, and my face, and body, and overall manliness are repeatedly anointed by the spray. Strong and stalwart, I gallantly endure it all, as I am battened down to whatever the hell it is you batten yourself down to.

And that's the problem, because in reality everything I know about boats you could fit on a Post-it. And even that paltry knowledge has been gleaned from movies and television—the captain always goes down with the ship; there is an apparent unspoken undercurrent of homosexuality in pirate culture.

For years I thought my lack of experience and education would forever disqualify me from my sailing adventure. I gave up and moved on to other things. Then, one summer I found myself back in Los Angeles with too much free time, and not nearly enough money. Earlier that year, a production company that dealt primarily in horror films had hired me to write a script for them. They were hoping to capitalize on the zombie craze that was currently sweeping through pop culture, but felt that they needed a different approach, something viewers hadn't seen before. In their infinite wisdom, the producers landed on Nazis to provide this novelty, and so I spent the next five months writing about the Third Reich's ability to raise the dead. I'd send in pages, only to receive emails with subject headings like Creativity vs. Historical Accuracy that began, *We are concerned about the liberties you're taking with the Zombie Goebbels character.* While that job was creatively soul crushing, it did mean that I didn't have to work over the summer. If I was conservative in my spending, I could stretch my Nazi necromancer money until September.

Unfortunately, my frugal intentions lasted about two weeks. I had too much free time, and to fill the days I'd go out to eat, or to bars. I'd go shopping, buying things I didn't need or even really want. I was burning through cash like a disaffiliated Mormon in Bangkok. Something had to be done. I needed a project that was time consuming, but with low overhead. As in so many moments of desperation, I turned to the Internet. I joined sailing websites and created profiles. I scoured the "Crew Wanted" pages and carefully drafted numerous responses explaining that my positive attitude, and ability to learn, more than made up for my complete and total lack of experience. I received dozens of polite responses from people wishing me well, but ultimately saying no. Then one morning I received an acceptance. This is how I met David.

"So, tell me what he's like?" my mother asked when I first called to tell her the details.

"I don't know," I said. "We've emailed back and forth a few times and spoken once. He seems like a nice enough guy."

"Yeah, that's how they get you."

"What? Besides, I'll be able to get to know him before I really commit to anything." I explained that David's boat was docked in a marina outside of Seattle. The plan was I'd use my miles to fly up and help him prep the boat for a few days, and then we'd sail to San Francisco, which would take another seven to nine days depending on the wind.

"And tell me," my mother continued, and I knew exactly where this was headed. "How old is this David?"

"Fifty-three."

"And it's going to be just the two of you? Out in a boat, in the middle of God knows where?"

"Yes, but…"

"Oh my God," she said, sighing deeply into her end of the phone. "Well, I hope you enjoy being molested."

Now there are two reasons why my mother would say this. First, she is convinced that the Internet is nothing more than a virtual bathhouse, populated by all types of perverts and deviants. This is in part due to her obsession with the *Dateline* exposé *To Catch a Predator*. In it, producers of the show pose as children in Internet chat rooms, hoping to attract and snare a would-be molester. At some point in the conversation, the toddler-toucher suggests a rendezvous, usually when the kid will be home alone, and the "child" agrees. It was here, waiting for the "ah-ha" moment when Chris Hanson and his camera crew would come bursting in, crashing the pervert's play date, that my mother would scoot to the edge of the couch, clench her fists, and shout towards the television "Yes! Gotcha sicko."

The other reason is that my mother finds me highly rapeable. No. Wait. That's a terrible way to phrase that. What I mean is that in these kinds of situations—me in an unfamiliar place, with unfamiliar people (men), my being molested is almost a foregone conclusion. In her mind I am a pederast's pin-up model, the apple of their wandering eye. Though this belief system hit its peak when I was a child—everyone was a possible suspect, every hand potentially menacing—it still continues to this day, despite the fact that I am thirty-five.

"I'm not going to get molested," I told her. "People do things like this all the time." I tried to explain to her the subculture of sailing. How there were hundreds of people out there who either had boats and needed help getting them from A to B, or else they were looking for some sailing experience and a possible adventure. This helped, but only so far for my mother to downgrade David from a pervert to a homosexual.

"Why not?" she said. "He recruits a good-looking young man to help him on his boat, and then sails him off to *San Francisco*. Think about it."

"That's the dumbest thing I've ever heard."

"Okay, then tell me Mr. Smarty Pants, what's the name of the website where you two met?"

"Cruisers Forum."

"Oh sweet Jesus!"

I told my mother that I had spoken to David on the phone, which was true, but if she knew the details of that conversation, her hysteria would have risen to a whole new level. It began innocently enough. We talked about where we lived, past jobs and current interests. David told me about his boat. At first he offered simple concepts, its size and age, but he soon delved deeper and deeper into technical specifications. I reminded him, as I had done in our previous emails, that I knew nothing about boats, but he either didn't hear me, or chose not to.

"Right now I'm runnin' a batten-less mainsail with a high aspect rig, but I'm thinking about converting to a fully battened sail. I figure that a significant roach would either require I reduce my luff or attach the bottom end of the backstay to a boomkin." Then he would pause, as if waiting for my sage wisdom and advice. I had no idea what he was talking about. The only words I caught were "significant roach," and I pictured a bug sporting a power suit and $200 haircut addressing a board of directors, which is probably not what he meant.

"Yeah, that sounds great." I'd say. "That's just how I'd do it."

Afterwards, he told me about his life. He'd been living alone aboard his boat for the last five years, bouncing around marinas in the Pacific Northwest. Once we got to San Francisco, he was going to pick up some more crew, and eventually make his way to Panama where he planned to retire.

"You're probably wonderin' how I can afford to do this," he said.

It hadn't crossed my mind, but as soon as he brought it up I was curious.

"Insurance money," he said. "There was a car accident. A head-on collision."

"Oh."

"I went through the windshield."

"OH."

"It wasn't too bad, no broken bones, or major lacerations."

"Well," I said, "that's good."

"Yeah, just some frontal lobe damage. No big deal."

And that's how he said it, like a casual aside, apropos of nothing, as if that were the most natural and expected continuation of his story.

I went to the mall for a soft pretzel, but they were out of the cinnamon sugars, so I killed the fat girl behind the counter and burned down the store. No big deal.

If I had bothered to research the effects of front lobe damage before I left, I would have learned that victims often suffer from an inability to make good choices or recognize consequences. They become irritable, and have difficulty regulating their behavior. I would have learned that the frontal lobe is responsible for something called "executive function," which controls planning, goal selection, self-monitoring, and self-correction.

But I didn't do that. Over the years I've found that things like knowledge and experience threaten the stability of my delicately constructed fantasies. They make poor bedfellows. Myopic, reality-eschewing laziness is what makes the fake world go round, and I wasn't about to let the details of David's busted brain ruin that for me.

I left for Seattle the next morning.

To meet up with David I had to take the monorail from the airport to downtown, getting off just south of Pike Place Market. From there it was a short walk to Pier 52, where I'd board a ferry for Bainbridge Island. Once there, two buses would take me to Port Ludlow and the marina where David's boat was docked.

"You'll transfer buses in the town of Poulsbo," David had told me in an email. "Give me a call when you get there."

Getting off the bus I thought the word "town" was a bit generous, as Poulsbo seemed to consist of nothing more than a small highway and thousands of pine trees. Even the bus stop was just an old bench and a laminated bus schedule nailed to a telephone pole.

Before I left, I had attempted to correctly program David's name and number into my phone. His last name begins with an E, but is then followed by an orgy of consonants, forming something that I can't pronounce much less spell. In the end I gave up, and he was entered as "David Boat Guy." He answered on the fifth ring.

"Hello."

"Hey David."

"Hello."

"David, it's me. The guy you're going sailing with."

"Right. How are you? What's going on?"

"I'm in Poulsbo, but I think this schedule must be wrong. It says the next bus doesn't leave until four thirty."

"No, that's right. There's only four buses a day in and out of Port Ludlow. That's why I wanted you to call."

"Oh, okay. So, what, are you coming to pick me up?"

"No. No, can't do that. Don't have a car."

"So you just wanted me to call, from the bus stop, to tell me that there wouldn't be another bus for," and I stopped to check the time, "three and half hours?"

"Uh huh."

"Alright. I'll see you in a while then," I said, hanging up. Why David thought I would want to bide my time in the middle of nowhere, instead of say, downtown Seattle, was a mystery. It would be the first of many.

I wandered around, looking for something to do, but all I found was a mini strip mall consisting of a store that sold prosthetic limbs and a Lane Bryant. As I was fully appendaged and not in the market for size twenty-two Capri pants, I hiked a few miles up the road until I found a Mexican restaurant. For three hours I sipped watered-down margaritas and ate stale chips and salsa and wondered if this is how all great sailing adventures begin.

The last bus dropped me off at the top of a small hill that offered a perfect view of my home for next few days. The Port Ludlow Marina was tucked into a small cove, surrounded on three sides by rolling hills of thick, evergreen woods. About two hundred or so boats were docked, bobbing gently on the calm, sun-dappled waters of Port Ludlow Bay. A snow-peaked Mount Olympus towered in the distance. *Okay*, I thought, *this is pretty good*. I saw David waiting for me at the base of the hill.

There had been a picture included with his Cruisers Forum profile, but it was taken from a distance, so I didn't know exactly what to expect. David had long, stringy black hair pulled back in a ponytail, and he was wearing a black T-shirt and acid-washed jeans the color of cloudless summer sky. I thought he looked younger than his fifty-three years, like a former roadie for Metallica. He would have rated about a five-and-a-half on my mother's potential pervert scale.

We shook hands, made the compulsory "how was your trip" chit-chat, and then headed towards the docks. When David turned, I saw what looked like a giant ice pick hanging from his belt. His pervert rating skyrocketed to a ten. *That's it*, I thought. *That's what he's going to hold to my throat as he slowly strips away my innocence*. I would later learn that it is called a marlinspike, a tool used to splice marine rope and untie knots. Still, I kept my eye on it.

David gave me a quick tour, showing me the bathrooms (or shore heads), showers and laundry room. The Port Ludlow Marina was home to a wide array of boats, and as we walked to David's, I saw sleek mega-yachts that were practically dripping with wealth and luxury, little schooners and single-person dinghies, and of course every make and manner of sailboat.

We must have been close, because David stopped and said, "Guess which one is mine."

For the record, I hate the guessing game. There are no real ways to win, just varying degrees of insult and embarrassment for both the guesser and guessee. As a child my Christmases were plagued by a visit from my Aunt Pauline, a penny-pinching cheapskate of the highest order. She would arrive at our house, unannounced, just in time for breakfast. After her third helping, she'd pull a present out of her giant old lady purse and force me to guess what it was. I, at first unaware of her extreme frugality, would suggest something normal, like a toy or video game. This was met by a look of wounded shame on Pauline's face, and horrific outrage on my mother's, as if I had just stood up and peed on the nativity scene.

In the intervening years I learned it was best to guess low enough so that the reality was not overmatched, but not so low as to be insulting. It helped that Pauline's gift to me never changed—a book of McDonald's coupons and a bag of airline peanuts. I also learned that Pauline's true gift to me was the unshakable belief that she would spend eternity burning in the hottest corners of Hell.

I surveyed the boats and selected a cream-colored sailboat with teak accents. It seemed like a fine specimen of wind-powered transport. Clean, classy, but not ostentatious. "Is it this one?" I asked.

"What?" David said, shaking his head in a wide-eyed look of disbelief. He reacted as if I had suggested he was the proud owner of a gold-plated hovercraft. "You're crazy," he said. "Just crazy."

David's actual sailboat was in fact a boat, but only in the same way that an 85 Buick, parked on blocks and slowly rusting out in some meth head's front yard is, technically, still a car. It had all of the basic parts—sides and a back, pointy bit at the front. It had a mast. It floated. But aside from that, this thing looked no more ready to sail to San

Francisco than the soda machine beside the bathrooms.

"So, what do you think?" David asked.

"You know," I said, "I had something in mind before I got here. But this, this doesn't even come close to that."

"Right? She's a real beauty, that little lady. Sure, she's getting on in years, but I still love her."

I admired the sentiment. Really, I did. The loyalty and devotion to something so cherished was rare, and it was refreshing to witness. But it has its limits. I could have said the exact same lovely things about my Grandma Bubby, but still, I'd never delude myself into thinking she was fit enough for a stranger to ride her all the way down to San Francisco.

We climbed aboard, and I decided to make the best of it. David said the boat would be ready to leave in a few days, and so I put my trust and faith in him. Plus, I figured, how much worse could it possibly get?

"Are you ready to see inside?" he asked.

We descended a small ladder into the cabin, which was the length and width of a bathroom stall. People have been buried in spaces with more square footage. To the immediate left was a single bunk, and to the right a shelving unit filled with all manners of trash: disposable razors, empty cans of food, deodorant sticks, and moldy jars of spaghetti sauce. And scattered among them all was an alarming number of prescription pill bottles. A low, foul odor hung in the air. It was the heady concoction of stale body odor and microwaved squash. Behind me was the kitchen, or galley. Crusted, broken-handled pots and pans filled the sink, and the small, retractable stove was coated in a layer of grease so thick I could have traced designs in it. Though there was enough headroom for David to stand easily, I had to crouch down to keep from rapping my head against the ceiling.

"What's this way?" I asked, hump-backing my way to the front part of the cabin.

"That's the forward cabin. There used to be another bunk in there, but right now I'm using it for storage."

Beyond the mast, the walls of the cabin gradually came together, forming the V that made of the bow of the boat. It looked like it could have been a warm, cozy little nook, but it was impossible to tell as this space was also drowning in trash. Milk crates crammed with tools were stacked at precarious angles, threatening to spill their contents with the slightest movement. Scraps of metal and lumber poked out from beneath leaking trash bags and piles of clothes. A plastic bin rested atop a heap of blue, dirt-caked tarps, and though I couldn't see inside, I was positive it contained pizza boxes filled with cat skeletons.

This was not what I had in mind. I was supposed to sail out into the open ocean, commune with nature, and bask in her many splendors. And, if Mother Nature demanded a price for such experiences, and threw me a storm, or sent rough waters my way, I would meet them head-on, my courage tested, my resolve strengthened.

But here, on this floating junk drawer, my biggest challenge would be not getting buried under an avalanche of hammers and sweatpants, or contracting hepatitis B. I had signed up for adventure on the high seas, but instead found myself on the nautical version of *Hoarders*.

"David," I asked, "where am I supposed to sleep?"

In anticipation of my arrival, David had installed a couple of hooks at each end of the cabin and rigged up a hammock. When unfurled, it hung right next to his bunk. We would sleep side by side.

"This'll do for now," he told me, "but once we hit open water, you'll need something more stable. I figure then, we'll just hot bunk it."

Okay, two things here. First, and call me old-fashioned, but of all of the sensations to be shared by two strangers, two male strangers, it seems that heat should occur a bit later in the relationship. Perhaps after a nice fondue dinner, and evening of musical theater. And second, although I didn't know what hot bunk meant, I didn't like that it was a verb. I don't want to be bunked by anybody, hot or cold.

It turned out that once David and I reached the ocean, one of us would have to do night watches to make sure we stayed on course. This meant that we'd sleep in shifts and could therefore share the bunk. The "hot" I guessed referred to the residual body heat we'd each feel as we changed shifts and climbed into bed. The reality wasn't as prison-rapey as I had imagined, but the thought still made me more than a little sick to my stomach.

"So, you ready for dinner?" David asked.

Dinner was actually a fairly decent meal of fish stuffed with crab served on a bed of brown rice. David said he wanted to make something special for my first night, and we ate on the deck of the boat, just as the sun slipped behind the pines. We made the usual small talk and discussed how in the morning we'd take the bus into town, have breakfast, and get some supplies to begin prepping the boat. At some point, our conversation veered towards David's current bout with kidney stones, and the medicine and copious amounts of cranberry juice prescribed by his doctor.

"I'm supposed to drink like a jug a day," he told me, "But it's tough. That and the pills got me pissing every ten minutes."

I thought, given our limited time together, and the fact that we were eating, that perhaps David's urinary adventures weren't the best topics of conversation. But I was a guest, so I sympathetically nodded my head. We continued eating, mercifully in silence, when David quickly sat up; shoulders back, spine rigid, the look on his face like a lightning bolt of panic. It was the kind of look people get when they're two hundred miles into a road trip and suddenly realize they've left the oven on.

"Something embarrassing has happened," David told me, though his eyes never found mine. "I think I have to go to the shore head." He gently set down his plate, rose, and left the boat. And as he walked down the docks toward the bathrooms, I saw a brown stain slowly bloom in the seat of his jeans, blighting their pristine, acid-washed blue.

Now it wasn't the act itself that bothered me. It happens. To everyone. You show me an adult that claims to have never shit themselves, and I'll show you a liar. It was just the timing of it. It was too much, and too soon. For some people, things like trust or respect have to be earned over a period time. For me, it's sympathy. If David had shit himself three or four days into our trip, no problem. But now, less than three hours from meeting him, and coupled with the fact that I'd be living in what was essentially a *Grey Gardens* linen closet, it was a lot to take in.

I assumed it was our dinner that had made David unwell, so I did what anyone in my situation would do—I threw it overboard. I figured it would sink, or that something would come along and eat it, but not only did dinner prove surprisingly buoyant, it seems that fish have reservations about cannibalism. To make matters worse, the current kept pushing the food towards the boat, gently rapping it against the hull. It was too far down for me to reach, so I frantically looked for a pole, or a stick, something I could use to break it up and make it sink. I thought how embarrassed I'd be if David returned, only to find his "special dinner" floating in the bay. Then, it didn't dawn on me that even though I had just witnessed a grown man shit himself in front of a stranger, I was the one concerned about losing face.

David returned a few minutes later, and found me on the deck, all smiles, a clean plate in front of me, the picture of a respectful guest. I had found an old, broken antenna, and used it to scoot the evidence to the far side of the boat.

"I'm not feeling too well," he said as he picked up his dish. "You can have this." And then he dumped the remains of his dinner on my plate.

Oftentimes on boats, their design and the objects within are created to be multi-purposed. This nod to complete yet varied functionality is meant to capitalize on the limited space. Deck chairs are also flotation devices. Tables fold down or extend from walls, making room for eating or navigation. Sometimes seats pull out, creating extra berths. David was also an advocate of this dual-purpose philosophy, though in his own unique way. It was clear that the floor, or shelves, or really any flat surface would also double as a trash can. We would also use two old hunter-green motor oil jugs as our bathroom.

"Excuse me?" I asked when this was explained.

"Toilet's broken," David told me. "It's good for number twos, but you can't piss in it."

He went on to explain that for the time being the toilet was stuffed with peat moss, which allowed it to accept "twos" but nothing else. This was a degree of nautical voodoo that I didn't understand and wanted no part of.

"It's on the list to get fixed, but until then, we gotta use these," David said, holding aloft one of the jugs.

"What about the shore head at the marina? Does it close at night?"

"No, it's unlocked, but it's way over there."

"Way over there" was actually about two hundred yards from the boat, which seemed like a fair penance to pay to avoid pissing into a jug, much less having containers of my waste lying around an area the size of a tool shed.

"I'm going to keep mine here," David said, "next to the wall. It's the one on the right okay?"

"Yeah, that's good," I said. "We don't want to get them confused.

That would be disgusting."

Having settled that matter, we unfurled the hammock, and went to bed.

It was around midnight when the ooeeys began. The hammock folded in on itself when entered, which made it almost impossible to fall asleep. And so cocooned in my canvas Hell, I heard the shifting of limbs, the rustling of sheets, like David was fighting the bed. Then it would get quiet, and David would emit in two drawn-out, and breathy syllables, the word ooeey.

"Ooooeeeey."

Having muttered this godless noise, David would climb from his bed, turn on the lights, and go to the bathroom. What's important to understand however, what must be implicitly clear for you to appreciate all thirty-one flavors of this experience, was the layout of our sleeping arrangements. There was the left (port) side of the boat, which David's bunk was flush with, then me, taquitoed in my hammock directly beside him, then about ten inches of space, and then the right (starboard) wall. This meant that to go to the bathroom David would have to stand on his bunk, gain his balance, then throw a leg over me and onto the shelving unit to my right, regain his balance, and then dismount and answer nature's call. It was the second move, with his one foot on the bunk, and the other on the shelf, that was the harrowing part, because it meant that he was essentially straddling me for the eternal seconds it took him to regain his balance.

What made it worse was that David felt compelled to turn on the lights before this routine, even though there was plenty of ambient light. What his little boat lacked in space, or cleanliness, it made up for in wattage, because when David flipped the switch there was enough light to perform open heart surgery. This, of course, celebrated the nuances of every gory detail, including the fact that David liked to wear black, mesh, bikini-brief underwear to bed.

So there I was, swaddled in my hammock, being straddled by a half-naked man with a recent history of rectal failure. David's mesh underwear did nothing to hide him, but instead rendered his junk in these monochromatic hues of black and gray, so it was like watching a 1930's porno. Except in 3D. And about two feet from my face. And lit with enough juice to be seen from the moon.

David would then use the bathroom, which of course meant urinating in one of our multipurpose jugs. This was not the end of the routine however, because there was barely enough room for him to stand, much less execute such a delicate docking maneuver. So when he peed, his body pressed against mine. And when he finished, and shook out those last few drops, his forearm rubbed up and down against my thigh. Yes, it was through the hammock, but still. I remember thinking: *Doesn't he know that's me. Doesn't he realize that the resistance he feels, the friction created as he shakes off his urine, is because he is rubbing against my body?*

Maybe it's me. Perhaps I'm overly sensitive to accidental contact. I know that if I bump into a stranger on a bus, or brush against a woman on a crowded elevator, I apologize profusely, like a leper with a restraining order.

Either way, David did not share my sentiment, as the entire act was done in silence. No *I'm sorry's*, or *Isn't life crazy sometimes?* or *Welcome to sailing, bitch!* He just finished his business, and on his way back to bed, straddled me again. This time he did it in reverse, so I was afforded a view of David's monochromed ass, which things being what they were, was an improvement.

Had this been an isolated incident, I'd like to think I could have endured. But it was not to be. Throughout the night David got up to use the bathroom thirteen more times. Thirteen more times he rose and brought forth the blinding white light. And thirteen more times he straddled me, his meshed sword of Damocles hanging inches from my face. And thirteen more times I felt the weight and heat from his body as he slowly filled that jug. No, that's not quite accurate, because as his condition progressed, David was called to the toilet on a number of occasions. This offered a reprieve from the friction-filled number ones, but only just slightly. The toilet separated the main cabin from the forward cabin, which meant it was about two feet from where I lay and blocked by nothing more than the mast of the boat. Take both your hands, and touch thumbs and index fingers. That was roughly the circumference of the mast pole. That was all that obstructed me from David's numerous and disturbingly auditory trips to the toilet.

And every time, every time, David announced the beginning of this ritual with what came to be the verbal manifestation of his troubled tummy, the plea for relief from his bedeviled bowels—Ooeey.

Now I know little about boats, and even less about boat culture, but it seems to me that if your body is having a going-out-of-business sale, and everything is marked to go, and you have to get up fourteen times throughout the night to use the bathroom, and getting up means climbing over and temporarily straddling the person, the stranger, who is fear-feigning sleep next to you, then maybe, at some point, you might consider taking the outside bunk.

Did I voice this concern? Did I make my disbelief and subsequent outrage known? I did not. Even now I'm not sure why. I guess I wanted to believe that each time would be the last, or at some point David would offer what seemed to be the most obvious thing in the world. That with each moanful ooeey he would realize how bizarre and futile these hellish acrobatics were and offer to switch places. Or maybe after his fifth, or ninth trip to the toilet, I no longer desired to trade beds with a guy battling diarrhea.

Regardless, David and his bowels settled down for good around three a.m., but I had decided I was leaving long before that. I can compartmentalize most things, and what I can't I drown in alcohol, but the filth of the boat coupled with David's toiled-themed Cirque de Soleil extravaganza was more than my system could handle. The first bus out of Port Ludlow didn't leave until eight, but that was no good as David planned for us to catch the other bus going into town. I knew I had to leave, but even more than that, I knew I wasn't ready to explain why to David. There could be no awkward goodbyes as we waited for our respective buses, and any reasons for my leaving could only bring about a flood of bewildered outrage, or pitiful judgment. So I decided to do what I always do when encountered with a challenging situation whose resolution requires grace and diplomacy; I decided to run away.

I would wait until first light, collect my things, quietly slip off the boat, and leave the marina. I figured I'd just hike along the road towards Poulsbo until the first bus caught up with me. Then I'd take the ferry back to Seattle, check into a hotel with a proper bed and a working toilet, and take the longest, hottest shower of my life.

The hatch to the boat's cabin had a small window, so from three to five a.m. I lay in my hammock and stared at the mast and the little sliver of sky beyond it. The time crawled by. I'd turn on my phone, only to discover that the last hour amounted to nothing more than seven minutes. Dejected, I'd stare at the sky, trying to discern changes in color as proof of a rising sun. *It seems more of a charcoal gray now than the iron skillet black it was a few minutes ago.*

The sky began to lighten around five, so I peeled myself out of the hammock, and collected my things, trying not to knock over the jugs of urine, or more importantly, wake David. The latter proved impossible. I'm not the most ninja-esque person in the best of circumstances but slipping off that boat undetected was like sneaking out of two-man coffin.

"What time is it?" David asked, rolling over in response to the racket I was making.

"I'm just taking a shower. You go back to sleep." *You've had a long night of incontinence and mentally scarring a complete stranger.*

Once off the boat, my road to freedom consisted of a two-lane blacktop that rose and fell through a thick evergreen forest. I figured David would sleep until seven, which gave me a two-hour head start before he realized I had fled. For a while I had the road to myself. I was up before most people left for work, so there were no cars, just the sound of the breeze through the pines, the birds chirping, and my feet on the asphalt. Alone with only my thoughts, I tried to assess the situation. I'd met a man on the Internet, and even though I knew little about him, I went to his place and spent the night. And now here I was, fleeing through the woods, after what was essentially a terrible one-night stand. I felt like at thirty-five I was finally learning a lesson most people realize when they're twenty-two.

Before I left LA David advised me to pack light, so I only had a small duffel bag and a backpack, the latter containing not much more than Cliff bars and bottled water. As the sun rose, so did the temperature, and before long sweat was running in my eyes, pooling in my lower back. My hand carrying the duffel bag would cramp up, so I'd switch it to the other one, but then that one would cramp up too. For a while, just to mix things up, I walked with the bag cradled to my chest, like a mother with her young child. I felt like a refugee. I had been persecuted, forced from my temporary homeland by unspeakable, inhumane acts. And now here I was, alone, braving the elements, protecting the few possessions I was able to salvage from my escape. I was like one of those Sudanese Lost Boys. *Yeah*, I thought. *That's exactly who I am.* Then I ate a Cliff Bar, had a few sips of Fiji water, and continued on.

By eight o'clock I was exhausted. There was still no bus, but I had been awake all night, and walking for the last three hours, so when I came upon the bus stop, I decided to sit and wait. At the sound of every car I'd crane my neck, and stare down the road, hoping to see the big, beautiful machine that would take me away. After about thirty minutes, I saw it slowly lumbering towards me. Newly revived, I jumped to my feet, already imagining myself back in Seattle. The bus rolled to a stop, its doors slowly accordioned open, and sitting right there, directly in front of me, was David.

"Hello there."

You know how in almost every horror film there is the scene where the young girl finally frees herself from her bonds, and escapes from the abandoned asylum, or madman's mansion, or whatever locale was serving as her inevitable demise? She goes tearing through the woods, only to come upon a small, country road. Then a car approaches, its headlights visible as it crests the rise of a hill. The girl jumps up and down, frantically screams and waves, imploring the car to stop. When it does, she runs around to the driver's side window, crying, pleading for help, explaining how there is a psychopath nearby, and she's got to get out of there. The window slowly lowers, and she sees that the person driving the car is the very same lunatic she's been running away from.

That is exactly what happened to me. I had become that young girl.

"There you are," David said. "What happened? You're not trying to leave are you?"

I just stood before the entrance to the bus. Shock, and fear, and disbelief vied for control of my body. I had made a wrong turn. In most situations I have a terrible sense of direction, but with the island's little signage, and all of those stupid, identical pine trees, I was doomed. Instead of going left out of the marina, towards Seattle, and salvation, and working toilets graciously surrounded by walls and locked doors, I went right. For three hours I hiked in the wrong direction, and it had taken David thirty minutes to catch up with me. In the end, utter defeat won out, and I climbed on the bus. I told David some bullshit story about looking for a coffee shop and getting lost. How at some point I'd gone so far that I figured he and the bus would just catch up with me.

"But why do you have all of your stuff?" David asked.

There were about five other people on that bus who has stopped whatever it was they were doing, now completely engaged in our little drama. They, like David, sat there, waiting for my answer.

"I...didn't want to wake you up bringing it back to the boat."

It was such an awful, transparent lie. I knew David wouldn't buy it. He would push me for the truth that I was too much of a coward to admit on my own. It would be awkward, and uncomfortable, but we'd get to the heart of the matter, and with our incompatibility fully exposed, I'd be free to go.

At first, David didn't say anything. He just stared at me with this look on his face. It was the kind of look people get when they're trying to do math in their head.

"Okay," he finally said. "So, what do you feel like for breakfast?"

And that was all that was said about it. I couldn't believe it. How could he just let it go? Why didn't he ask for a further explanation? In the end I decided not to push my luck and sat in the seat next to him. I figured that for the first time since I had arrived, David's brain damage was working in my favor, and if I didn't have to volunteer my motives, especially on that bus, filled as it was with kindly small-town folk, then so be it. I knew that my calm, quiet reasons would immediately devolve into loud, harsh criticisms. I'd turn to the passengers, seeking acceptance and validation. *Fourteen times*, I'd yell. *Jugs of urine*,

I'd explain, but they wouldn't understand. They'd see me as the crude, sanctimonious out-of-towner, who was unwilling to appreciate the unique characteristics of one of their own. They'd turn on me, and likely run me out of town. Don't get me wrong, I still wanted to leave, but I wanted it to be on my terms.

David and I ate at the Blue Moose Café, a squat, greasy spoon perched in the middle of a shipyard. The place was packed, and when we entered all the sailors and shipbuilders turned to stare at David, and what looked like some wayward runaway he picked up on his way to breakfast, which was pretty much what I was. We had to sit at the counter, with my bags piled beneath my feet like so much shame. For the most part our meal transpired with the relaxed, carefree manner of an arranged marriage. I picked at my blueberry pancakes and sucked down multiple cups of coffee trying to stay awake. David made attempts at conversation, discussing our plans to get some supplies and things for dinner, but I wasn't in the mood for chitchat.

"I hope we have time to get everything finished before the eleven o'clock bus," David said. "If we miss it, then we'll have to wait until three. We'll be trapped here, and we certainly don't want that."

I turned from my plate and looked at David for the first time since we had sat down. "No," I said. "We certainly don't."

David and I picked up what we needed and returned to the marina with a plan. We'd spend the rest of the day preparing the boat and making necessary repairs. I found myself newly invigorated about the whole idea. Little by little David and I would make progress. I'd see the effects of our efforts, and perhaps along the way, I'd explain how it was socially frowned upon for people to poop in front of one another. On the way back I had told David I could no longer sleep in the hammock, blaming it on a preference to sleep on my stomach, and not on having his diarrheic bottom dangled in my face all night long. He agreed to switch bunks. With the sleeping situation taken care of, I figured if I spent the next solid thirty hours scrubbing the boat clean, it could pass as livable. I could stick this out and still get my sailing adventure. The first night was an anomaly, I told myself. How much worse could it possibly get?

"Okay," David said. "First thing we'll do is install the new brushed-nickel hardware for the cabinets. Then, we'll sand and varnish the tiger wood casing for the compass."

Since I had arrived David had been boasting about these cosmetic upgrades. *Hardware*, I thought. *Compass housing?* How about we install a door, or a piece of plywood, or an Elmo beach towel, anything to separate the bathroom from the rest of the cabin so I don't have to watch you ooeey into the toilet fourteen times a night? Shouldn't that be on the top of the to-do list?

I felt my resolve weakening. David went into the forward cabin, returning with a pair of his tool-filled milk crates. Then he dumped each of their rusty, greasy remains on his bed. Now my bed. From the debris emerged a cockroach that quickly scrambled over hammers, and under screwdrivers. David grabbed a set of needle-nose pliers, impaling him. I felt sorry for the little creature. He was no doubt just looking for a cleaner, and more hospitable environment. I felt sorry for him until David wiped his puss-oozing carcass on the pillowcase, my pillowcase, and then I went back to feeling sorry for myself.

We spent the rest of the day making David's cosmetic improvements. I tried suggesting more pertinent repairs, but these were met with a look of curious bewilderment, and then shot down.

"So," I said, "what do you think we should work on after this? The toilet maybe?"

"No. I think we'll run the wiring for the digital GPS."

"Yeah," I said, "that's a good idea." *That way, when I'm watching you piss into a jug all night long, I'll know exactly where I am.*

Because of the limited space, and the nature of the work, even our cosmetic improvements were a one-man job. I spent the majority of the day just standing in the cabin, handing David the odd tool like a despondent nurse. David's handyman abilities proved just a notch above his housekeeping talents. It took most of the afternoon for him to install the hinges and pulls for the cabinets, and he cracked the first two pieces of tiger wood for the compass housing. This meant that he had to saw all new pieces, which of course he did on the bed.

At one point I remember standing in the cabin, looking around, ignoring David's frustrated pleas towards some uncooperative piece of hardware. My gaze landed on some stains on the wall. Some unholy cocktail of grease and liquid rust had dripped down from its holds and created a pattern of shapes just below the cooler. One looked like an Egyptian hieroglyphic of a man. Beside it, two long streaks came together, forming a V, and beneath it a loose oval. *That one looks like the head of bunny,* I thought.

And then it spoke to me.

"What the hell are you doing?" it said. "Standing here like an ass-clown, finding shapes in the filth like they're clouds on a picnic day. This boat is a shitpit, and David either doesn't realize it or care, and nothing you can do will change that. Besides, at the rate you two are going, this thing isn't going to be ready to sail until the next decade."

That dirty bunny was right. This was ridiculous. I had to get out of there. I resolved to try again. In the morning I would sneak away, and this time confident in the directions, I would return to Seattle. That night I went to sleep in my bed of sawdust and cockroach remains, and at sunrise I slipped away.

Then, I didn't explain my reasons for leaving, and I still haven't.

Hours after I left David began calling, and this continued for the next few days. "David Boat Guy" would appear on my phone, but every time it was ignored. I know I owe him an explanation, and perhaps one day he'll get it. I can say that the morning I left, David was asleep in the hammock beside me, which meant I had to straddle him on the way out. I accidently woke him up, but I purposefully stood over him for an extra beat, letting my ass linger in his face. It was my way of saying goodbye, and for now it will have to suffice.

Thanks to Diane Goettel for plucking this odd assortment of stories from the slush, and everyone at Black Lawrence for helping me turn it into a book. Thanks to Deb Weiers for your brilliant cover art. Thanks to the Texas Tech Graduate School for your monetary support and recognition that visiting an amusement park or attending a summer camp can, in fact, be research. Thanks to Jill Patterson for your friendship and mentorship. For introducing me to a unique camp in upstate New York, and for what is, to this day, the best colostomy bag anecdote I have ever heard. Thanks to Curtis Bauer and Katie Cortese for helping me strengthen and shape this thing when it was in its rawest form. Thanks to my Lubbock friends: Eric, Chase, Robby, Mike, Jess, and Kates. Thanks to the Dennises, big and little, for your interest in and enthusiasm for these stories. And finally, thanks to Gatsby and Jill Fennell for my many months at the Fennell Writer's Residency and its myriad perks.

Thanks also to the editors and journals who first published these stories:

"Camp Vampire Kids," *Philadelphia Stories,* Fall 2019

"Boat Guy," *Cahoodaloodaling,* Issue #23, Spring 2017

"Cry on Command," *The Lascaux Review,* The Lascaux Prize Anthology, 2017

"Endangered Animal Release Specialists," *American Fiction, Vol. 15,* 2017

"The Reluctant Son of a Fake Hero," *Carve Magazine, Premium Edition Issue,* 2016

"The Continuing Controversy of the Snuggle Shack," *Master's Review, Vol. IV,* 2015

JOE DORNICH is a graduate of Texas Tech's creative writing program where he was the managing editor of *Iron Horse Literary Review*. His stories have won contests and fellowships from *The Master's Review*, *Carve Magazine*, South Central MLA, Key West Literary Seminars, and the South Carolina Academy of Authors. Joe lives in Knoxville and teaches at the University of Tennessee.

www.ingramcontent.com/pod-product-compliance
Lightning Source LLC
Chambersburg PA
CBHW030609310726
48979CB00003B/636
* 9 7 8 1 6 2 5 5 7 1 3 2 8 *